THE FAT PRINCESS

My parents used to live a fairy-tale existence.
I've always found fairy tales to be mind-numbing. That fact hasn't escaped my parents' notice, which is why they read me one every night. To knock me out.

I'm a bundle of words. My mind is riddled with all the sentences playing peas porridge hot, pat-a-cake, pat-a-cake, and Peter Piper up there, running in one ear and tripping out my tongue.
I always repeat everything I hear.

My dad and mom like to hold me close and tell me all kinds of stories, many revolving around their lives, which I overrun. I invade their eyes, their ears, and their mouths. I demand enormous amounts of attention and concentration. They devote mind and patter to finding sensical answers to the nonsensical questions their adventures inspire in me. Curiosity demands that I dot every j, cross every t, never minding my P's and Q's. I try to stump them daily, each question tougher than the next, no topic taboo. Sometimes I rephrase the questions a few days later just to see whether they've changed their story; sometimes I just forget.

My dad is the king of storytelling and my mom's the dictionary queen; together they've managed to make a right colourful parrot out of me. Of course, I'm not really a parrot. No evil witch has cast a spell on me. I'm just a little girl whose colourful language extends to words such as psittacism, borborygmus, and the like. My head reels from so many words of all shapes and sizes – they congest my lungs and must be regularly expelled. My liver is backed up with them, my stomach all bloated from the words it retains. I let loose the occasional borborygmus; my native tongue has reached a bombastic state. I will never be cured. It's all the fault of my vocabulary.

I have a serious illness since my parents say it's in my blood. Everything I hear, I'm capable of repeating word for word. I probably get that from my dad. My dad keeps trotting out the same old sayings day after day, the tiredest of all being, "What do you say?" I guess "thank you" must be too small a phrase for me to retain; my memory is like a sieve.

However, my blood circulation is good, although the earthy language in my system leads to some congestion of the brain, not that I run a fever, I run on sentences instead.

My parents say I'm a genius, but they're wrong. I'm quite a run-of-the-mill little girl. I draw what I see and repeat what I hear. Mostly, I just talk all the time. To my father, in the main. Together, he and I make a team. We pass the buck; he runs interference for me. When I was little and ate mashed potatoes, he'd pick them up off the floor, when I cry at night, he's up too, when I cross the street, he holds my hand. I'm quite a handful, you know. My every action is accompanied by a word: I often talk with my mouth full, when I cry I blubber incoherently, and I comment on everyone we pass in the street.

I'm forever talking. When I doodle on my dad's writing paper, he swears he'll write a story about me. He gives his word, but I can't tell whether he's writing what I say or what he thinks. Because I can't read. What kind of genie of us does that make me? Besides which, I don't have any magic powers, I've never been trapped alive inside a lamp, and I'm not a thousand years old!

If you really must know, I'm not quite five and not the least bit fat!

I am, however, a true-to-life princess. I know that for a fact because of my huge verdoyant kingdom and my magnificent blue coach.

THE KINGDOM

For the most part, my kingdom consists of vegetation, and my subjects vegetate. That's because I reign over Carré St. Louis.

Carré St. Louis is frequented by aimless ne'er-do-wells ne'ering and welling their lives away. My vassals lose themselves in daydreams, stare at the fountain, inhale the fragrant flowers or, for those still capable of love, lock lips in an embrace. Worst of all, some of the loners read.

Reading puts me to sleep!

In fact, I'm even thinking of banning books in my park, just like any other drug....

It goes without saying that my domain is unfortified. Its borders wouldn't be crossed so easily otherwise! I would have them sealed shut. Instead of scattered benches too high for me to climb, I'd surround my park with unscalable walls.

The many benches I own are constantly under siege by the enemy come from neighbouring districts and lands. For the most part, the enemies are fierce grown-ups, and I'm powerless against those bums.

One corner of my park sports bizarre metal sculptures. I give them a wide berth because they're such a fright. Art can be like that – scary, you know.

That's not all. The harmless lampposts scattered throughout my territory have also begun to strike fear in me ever since my dad started reading me the story of Don Quixote. Who knows, maybe they breathe fire after dark.

There are all kinds of adventures to be had in my kingdom. It's a royal blast. With my dad anything's possible.

The catch is there are no swings, no sandpiles, no slides. Nothing to play with, in fact. You have to give your imagination free rein to have fun.

All summer long, though, there is the wading pool. Grown-ups stay clear, not for fear of ridicule but for fear of the vile water! The huge fountain I've already mentioned rises up smack in the middle of the pool. Someone told me the fountain is lit up at night, which I myself can't vouch for, but it comes from a reliable source.

Anyway, I'm always in bed by that time. I go to bed early. Too early if you ask me.

Naturally, my park is full of trees and flowers. If there weren't any flowers, it wouldn't be my park.

At home, we have all kinds of plants. Inside and out. I love their colours. A love of flowers is healthy. Like alternative medicine. To smell my garden is to be happy. In autumn, the trees are awesome. Later, I'll have a big vegetable patch.

This year in Carré St. Louis I took inventory of the geraniums, alyssum, pansies, and petunias –

commonly known as St. Joseph's flower, but don't ever let my parents hear you say that! The name is in no way scientific, it's biblical, which is worse.

There are also tuberous begonias, impatiens, ageratum, nicotine and, along the same lines, a significant number of cigarette butts. All proliferate gaily in the flowerbeds.

Flowers are all well and good, but you're not allowed to pick them for fancy bouquets. Not that my mom ever complained when I brought a bouquet home to her, not until I told her where I'd handpicked the flowers, that is.

My mom is always scolding me for stealing flowers from Carré St. Louis. *Don't you think we have enough flowers in our own garden?* You can never have enough flowers if you ask me.

Anyway, flowers belong to everyone. We can all look at the flowers, smell the flowers, why not pick the flowers, too?

My mom has tried to impart what she calls *a proper sense of responsibility and respect for other people's property* to me. It sounds like a university course. Her lessons do get their point across, more or less. *Other people in the park won't be able to appreciate the beauty and perfume of the flowers if you pick them and bring them home.* She could be right.

But what's one to do once the harm's been done?

How can you part with flowers once they've been pulled out of the ground? It's not as though I can put them back. Gardening with cuttings is an art unto itself! What choice do I have? March to the police station and turn myself and the flowers in? I don't think so. I do know there's no way I can throw them into the garbage! Now that would qualify as a criminal act! So we put them in a jar full of water, and I'm warned not to repeat the offence.

*

Last but not least, the only building on my domain is a sanitary facility that doubles as my fortified castle, called urinal for short. Urinals were invented by Emperor Vespasian, that's his name carved into the lintel above my castle's door. Lintel is a real word, too. My dad teaches me all the words like urinal, even if they're a bit colourful for my age.

I won't beat around the bush. Urinal means a toilet for men.

Despite my gender and equipment, I too can pee standing. I'm a girl and haven't worn diapers in ages except at night. My mom doesn't like it when I pee standing up, but she's quite forgiving if I pee lying down while I'm asleep. It's a shame that the urge to pee doesn't wake me up. I hate to sleep but can't help myself. Could it be I'm scared?

Most of the time, though, I do all my business sitting down, which is better than nothing.

In my urinal, no one has stood to pee for ages because the building has been turned into a small snack bar. Sometimes my dad and I buy an almond croissant with a glass of milk; fruit juice is out of the question unless it's freshly squeezed. So are soft drinks, chocolate, cookies, and any sort of candy.

My dad flips out when it comes to food. He's a real despot. *Don't eat this and don't eat that* are the orders he barks most frequently. His dictatorship knows no bounds. One time after I'd wolfed down six or ten chocolate bars, he even made me throw up. That's nothing, though. Another time I overdid it, he pumped me full of antidotes. My dad's paranoia can turn quite ugly.

For now, my castle is fairly humble and small. But over the next few years, my lackeys will undoubtedly have enough time to build huge kitchens adjoining the present one, as well as deep dark dungeons, deep dark oubliettes, and machicolated towers. The surrounding roads will be excavated to form deep water-filled moats teeming with crocodiles, the stuff of horrific tales. Not to mention vast ballrooms and bedrooms that I'll have furnished with majestic beds topped by high canopies. No. Better yet there'll be neither bedroom nor bed, just huge playrooms in their stead!

In short, it will include everything that makes a castle real because one day I'll be queen. I am a princess after all.

And I'm not fat!

I can't stress that fact enough.

THE GARDEN

To show you just how no-fat I am, I have a string bean physique and a root vegetable nickname – "carrot top" – that my friends call me.

The fact is I don't belong to either the Papilonionacae family of leguminous plants or to the Umbelliferae family of root vegetables. I do belong to the Thébergirard family, and there's not a vegetable in sight. Just my parents. Or my roots, if you prefer.

If you had a mother like mine, you'd know every plant by both its names, its common name and its Latin name, as well as the families to which each one belongs. For instance, marigolds, those small, gorgeous yellow flowers, also answer to the name *calendula* and are members of the Compositae family. They're special in that they are wholly edible. My dad, however, who is not a poet and so quite insensitive to their beauty, is the only person I know capable of crushing them between his teeth without the slightest twinge of conscience. That's a novelist for you.

My mom's not a poet either, but her favourite hobbies are gardening and photography.

The fountain, the trees, the flowers, and a handful of old vegetables reading, dreaming, and loving are what makes up Carré St. Louis.

"Carré St. Louis…" I always pronounce those three words with great solemnity, like an incantation, and my park turns into a magic rectangle in which anything and everything is possible. I close my eyes for the space of a second, and instantly images flash through my head. Dreams more stupendous than anything I've ever come up with in bed.

Back when I was a baby, my mom would often bring me here for my afternoon nap. I slept in a buggy that my dad called a coach – erroneously – yet, at the same time, it was undeniable proof that in his eyes I've always been a princess.

In those bygone days, I was absolutely incapable of holding out against sleep. But those days are long past; I'm not such a pushover anymore, I know how to put up a fight. I'm a child of the video age and know all about mortal combat. Maxime, the friend I only see every other weekend, has two ultrarealistic electronic games where all the fights are in 3-D so the enemy is always being beaten to a pulp to the accompaniment of incredibly bright spurts of blood. I don't have any games to compare because of my parents' fierce opposition. My parents' ideas are old-fashioned, their games and books are just old.

Despite the modern era in which we live, my parents insist on reading me medieval stories, which I've learned to like all the same.

I love being read to, but I never forget that sleep lies in wait. Every night I'm ambushed no matter how high I put up my guard.

I fight off sleep in a merciless duel. My opponent is strong, and his accomplice is my father. My dad's voice is deep and soothing; his words resonate soundly off the anvil of my ears. His descriptions of battles between valiant knights and despicable scoundrels are reminiscent of the nightly war I wage on the sandman. At times his words are lost in the clamour of combat. Swords ring violently off each other and shields collide, making a constant racket not unlike my games with pots and pans. The sparks start to fly! Spears hit armoured mesh with a screech that sets your teeth on edge; sometimes long, pointed weapons nick an opponent's breast-plate. Once in a while, swords go right through hel-mets, in one thrust killing those men whose heads are still attached. Hostilities continue until the most villainous scoundrel of all penetrates the castle, makes off with the princess, no rescuer in sight, then…

The ending never changes – I'm overcome with sleep. That just slays me!

I hate to sleep. I'm afraid I'll never wake up. I'm invaded by dread seconds before I drop off.

Is it any wonder?

THE TRUTH

My dad says I'm going to die.

I know, I know, death is a subject that is better left to books for children. You should never discuss death in the presence of grown-ups, especially not grown-up grandparents because they're going to be faced with it sooner than the rest of us. For my part, I'm still fairly young so I don't mind talking about death.

I am going to die.

Now that may seem quite straightforward, but it's more complicated than you think. How should I explain it? I can't remember exactly how my dad's explanation went, but somehow I understood.

I won't exist anymore. Voilà. That's about it. I'm going to disappear for good. Like before, before I existed, before I was in my mom's tummy. Only this time I'll be dead. There'll be nothing left of me. Just pictures and some drawings.

The same goes for you, your friends, your family, everyone. One day, life just comes to an end, like that, and we'll be buried or burned or who knows what else. I have to confess it's kind of hard to stomach, especially for an adult. But you have to believe

me. That's the way life is, my dad said so, it's true.
I'm not making this up.

*

At the time my dad gave his explanation, I don't
think he had begun to worry about dying, at least
not in any real sense.

Any apprehension, however, has been rein-
forced since then, and now my dad knows his subject better, due to an actual brush he had with death.
A close one at that....

My mom's the one who wanted to do him in.

It all happened because I told her how my dad
said I was going to die.

Now I realize that I shouldn't have said a word.
I didn't know whether my mom knew what was
going to happen to me – and to her too one day – so
I decided to warn her in advance of the fate that
awaits us all.

My announcement came as a total shock to her.
I don't think she suspected a thing. My mom
hunched over, visibly saddened by my painful revelation. Not a word of a lie, she started to weep! Not
real sobs, but tears filled her lower lids, and some
even spilled over. I wasn't the least bit sad. I had to
comfort my poor mom so I hugged her real tight.
What else could I do? Tell her it wasn't true? Maybe,
but by then it was too late.

So my dad was right: adults fear death more
than kids do.

As my mom mopped her tears, she asked very
gently, "Who told you you're going to die,
princess?" And I said, "Daddy did."

I can't relate her response right here, I'm still too young, and there were too many new words strung together for me to be able to identify them clearly. Her gentleness of two seconds earlier had vanished without a trace. Her deep sorrow had been brutally transformed into seething rage and her hands to fists. She was furious! There could have been hell to pay. It was lucky my dad wasn't around. It saved his life, of that I'm convinced. She did say in front of me, "I'll kill him," but she doesn't have to go to all that trouble because my dad's going to die anyway, just like the rest of us.

*

These things always happen in royal families: at the slightest contretemps, they slip hemlock to their relatives in broad daylight or stab them in their sleep after the stroke of midnight.

Under the circumstances, how can a body be expected to sleep?

THE SHOE

I am a princess and I have a coach, but I'm no Cinderella.

I only have one shoe, but you can't see it because I hid it under my sweater.

I'm no Cinderella because the shoe doesn't fit my right foot, not even close. Or is it the left foot? I still have trouble telling which foot is which. In any case, my shoe is way too big for me. And even if it was a perfect fit, I wouldn't want to be Cinderella.

I only have one shoe, not because I lost the other one running around outside like most kids my age. It's a well-known fact that running is a no-no, even on the sidewalk, unless you really have to pee. And never run when crossing the street. You have to hold someone's hand. So, as I was saying, my other shoe isn't lying on the double line down the middle of a boulevard somewhere. No, it's lying in a shoe-box in the back of the store I stole it from.

Yes, you heard right, I stole a shoe.

It was so easy. The shoe was sitting on display, with no guard in sight.

I know it's bad to steal. But I'm not a good little girl. I'm not the kind of girl who'd wash someone else's floor all day without a word of complaint. I'm no Cinderella, that's for sure!

Or Nina Ricci either.

That's the name written inside the pump in my hand.

I thought the only place that made you write your name on your shoes was the nursery I go to and the kindergarten down the street. It would seem that the practice is much more widespread and that adults do the same thing. Refusing to grow up again…

My dad and I make a very important distinction between the nursery I go to and the kindergarten down the street where my friend Maxime goes and which I've never set foot in. There's no point explaining what the distinction is right now since I'll be going to my nursery on Monday, and you'll see for yourself.

But back to my shoe.

The reason I stole a shoe for grown-ups was to help my mother out of a bind. Since my dad's hurried departure, I must say that our financial situation has gone steadily downhill.

THE HEATED EXCHANGE

My parents used to live a real fairy-tale existence that ended abruptly the day I was born. Nothing was ever the same again. Especially during those first few months.

Every two or three hours, like clockwork, there'd be a heated exchange.

As soon as I'd start to cry, my dad would fetch me from my crib and take me to my mom who'd already started crying just thinking of what was to come, but I absolutely had to be fed. My dad didn't want me on the bottle, which is why I think my mom resented him so much.

Ergo the heated exchange.

I wasn't too gentle with my mom's breasts. I sucked on them voraciously with my hot hard gums. We're real suckers for the people we genuinely love. I was as greedy as a suckling calf, and my mom let me have my way. The maternal instinct is quite animalistic. That type of animosity just strengthens family ties.

For all the above reasons, my dad called nursing "the heated exchange." He was also trying to soothe my mom because her demolished nipples were horribly cracked, puckered, and chapped – the whole shebang. However, my dad's jokes only served to exasperate her further, which is easily understood.

I don't exchange that kind of heat with my mom anymore, and we understand each other better now that I've quit talking with my mouth full of milk.

I learned later in life that a mother's milk is the perfect antidote for viral infections so I guess everyone else in the nursery I go to must have been bottle-fed because they're always getting sick.

I've been sick since the day I was born. Day in, day out. I've never come down with hugely fatal illnesses, thank goodness, but I have had every contagious disease that makes the rounds at my nursery – typhoid fever, red measles, German measles, whooping cough and chicken pox – for solidarity's sake. I've also had tonsillitis and that *damnedotitis* an alarming number of times.

My dad has had it up to here with the latter attack on sensitive ears. The internal racket[1] drives him to use cotton balls.

I've tried every antibiotic flavour known to man as dispensed in every one of multiple forms – syrup, pills, suppositories – but shots work best of all. I happen to hate shots, which is my tough luck since I get them all the time.

I don't make a fuss about popping a pill, but boy do I hate to shoot up. I can guarantee I'll never be a junkie! Take my word for it. I have nothing against

---

1   "Infernal racket"? Correctrix's note.

sharing a little joint now and then with my dad, but no way will I ever inject my arms full of drugs. You have my word on that!

NIGHT-TIME

As I've mentioned already, fairy tales generally have the effect of an anesthetic on me despite my insatiable desire to be in full possession of my senses at all times. Drugs are one thing, but there isn't a sedative on earth as effective as Perrault's nursery tales.

I hate to sleep.

Yet I'm overcome by total paralysis even before being administered the prescribed dosage of pages.

I can't help myself, I doze off with each dose, especially during fairy tales.

Fairy tales invariably involve a mission. The heroine is always called upon to perform some extraordinary feat. To do so, she has to overcome what seem insurmountable obstacles, avoid treacherous traps, and jump through a whole series of other bureaucratic hoops.

Paperwork in general, printed forms of any kind, subtitled films, advertising pamphlets, children's books, and the lists of ingredients on food packages are the hurdles I have to clear. They give rise and fall to incredible ups and downs when I'm in their presence. My own secret mission is to learn how to read. I try to fulfill my mission while being read to in bed.

But I don't like my bed. Nor do I like bedtime stories, bedside manners, or diabetic shots. Or dandelions! A dandelion is not just another pretty yellow flower growing wild and a member, like calendula, of the Compositae family. It is also a leaf vegetable that enters into the composition of delicious salads for people who go in for that sort of thing. It's not the taste I hate, it's the lyin' part of dandelion. Anything to do with bed or with lying gives me the royal creeps.

I hate lying in my bed. My mattress, my mattress cover, my pillow and sheets all instill terror in me. Even my duvet, notwithstanding its varicoloured flower motif, gives me the willies. I hate my bedroom, but not because of its decorative motif. It might as well be black the way I feel. My bedroom is painted yellow, except for one wall papered in flowers (to match my duvet) to which I've added, with the help of felt markers, several other flower varieties, the long-blooming kind since they refuse to disappear no matter how hard they're scrubbed with soap. I can't stand my room because it is the theatre of my bed. I hate my bed – I hate its colour, its height and, above all, its width. It is so obscenely wide that one of my parents has room to sit down next to me as I'm lying there. That's when my story gets read.

Why is it that, historically, stories have always been read at bedtime? Why not in the morning? If only I could read to myself when and where I want!

I love my parents, but I hate to sleep, and their soft voices, warm and enveloping, whisk me away to the land of blinding moons.

I'm a restless sleeper. I have particularly bad dreams when my dad reads me *Tales for Naughty Children*. The storybook is by Jacques Prévert, and the author himself did the illustrations on every page. For the most part, they feature half-human, half-animal beings. Once sleep comes, all kinds of lugubrious creatures start to appear on my ceiling to mingle with Charles Perrault's characters.

I imagine wolf-soldiers, obese kings, cyclope sentinels, hyena attendants, vampire bats, evil fairies, the wife-killer Bluebeard, or the mute man who strangles the mute woman, probably for a lack of fidelity, or the blind archer who shoots blind arrows, most likely for the same reason. Men are cruel and evil, and the world's too dangerous for sleep. To stay alive, you need to stay awake.

I really hate to sleep.

At night all cats turn grey, while in the light of day our cats are a funny colour. It's hard to say exactly what. But I'd love to see them all decked out in grey.

We have two cats. Chlorophyll and Clarinette. Contrary to what you might think, Chlorophyll is not green, but he's always stretched out on the warm window sill in the sun. He's engaged in what my mom and I call photosynthesis. In other words, he likes sunlight, hence his name. I should also mention that he sometimes makes himself sick eating the leaves off the plants he sees, then throwing up everywhere. His throw-up, on the other hand, is green.

Clarinette just runs around knocking over most everything in her way, and that's that.

Two cats, both the same size, the same colour
Clarinette, a girlcat, and Chlorophyll, her
brother

That sounds like a nursery rhyme.

I hate nursery rhymes and not just because of the clumsy verse. They're slumbrous because they're sung. My mom's lullabies give me motion sickness, all that rocking back and forth. Whether sung or read aloud, stories don't seem to agree with me – they trigger a mysterious dizzy-making fever and force me into bed. How could I ever truly love something as soporific as nursery rhymes?

I hate poetry too! I don't like Prévert's books or other books that size. In fact, I make it a point to try to hate all things written because I don't know how to read. How can I love my mother tongue when it's both the source of incomparable beauty and battles too numerous to count?

SEPARATION

There are heated exchanges like the ones I described earlier, and then there are heated exchanges that are actual conflicts. When people can't go around killing each other with bombs, a surefire way to inflict injury is to target the other's mother tongue. With improper use, words can become cruel aggressors and spark conflicts with irreversible consequences.

In Quebec, French is one of the main arguments for separation. Take my parents, for example.

My father is a riter and my mother teaches French. My mom always used to correct the many huge mistakes my dad made in his novels, but it had a dramatic effect on their relationship.

Ever since I came on the scene, my mom hasn't had any time for you-know-what so my dad has other women do it for him, correctrixes for the most part.

What else do you expect? Only girls correct my father's books, which is only natural since girls are better than boys in French. In math too. And geography. When it comes right down to it, girls are better at everything. Boys are just plain dumb. Except my dad of course, because he's my dad.

My mom does have trouble accepting my dad's relationship with other women. Their intercourse can be a real trial. My dad has shown me a few examples and believe you me, those women are sadists through and through. They clearly like to inflict pain. I've never seen so many red lacerations on a sheet of paper, more even than on the exams my mom brings home from school. Not to mention all the unheard-of suffering that ensues on the home front.

Maybe my dad's a separatist, who knows? Many artists are; they often trade in spouses; they frequently divorce on a whim. Now the same holds true for the general population. I hope the fad will die out one day and that all those parents will start thinking of someone other than themselves.

Now don't get me wrong, I am for separation, except where children are involved. Unless, of course, women and children are being abused.

What's more, I think you should have to take out a licence to have a child.

You need a licence to drive a car, to renovate a bathroom, to play music in the subway, and you have to be eighteen to buy wine and cigarettes (I know because I've already tried), but if you're only twelve with twelve dollars to your name and twelve foster families in your past, it seems you can still go ahead and have a child.

And if you're thirty, with thirty credit cards, thirty comely co-workers – all of whom you will have laid before too long – and what would seem to be an intellectual quotient of thirty since you very

likely have a partner who loves you unquestion-
ingly, you can still get her pregnant and hightail it
out the next year.[2]

*

If there are mistakes in this book, and I sincerely
hope there are, it's because I asked my dad to prove
to me that he's no longer seeing a correctrix. If I
were to discover that my dad was still calling on
girls to correct his novels, I could never forgive him.

In the normal course of events then, this book
should be peppered with errors in spelling and
grammar. At least I would breathe easier if that was
the case. My problem is I can't read so there's no
way I can see for myself.

I'd like to ask my mom to help, but as I've
already mentioned, she doesn't have time for that.
Anyway, if my mom saw mistakes in French in her
Mario's book, she would be fit to be tied!

I should point out that my parents are not married. Mario is my dad's name.

My dad didn't want to ask for my mom's hand
before they had me on their hands, and now it's too
late.

---

2   I realize that I have somewhat overstepped my character's
parameters here. I promise not to do it again. Author's note.

THE TRAGEDY

My dad has gone.

As I mentioned earlier, since his departure our financial situation has gone steadily downhill.

Although my dad has gone, he didn't leave us for a correctrix and the things she does for him.

I still have my occasional doubts, but I like to think that my dad is faithful, not just to my mom but to a minimum number of grammatical, spelling, and literary conventions. Everyone is entitled to a few mistakes in their youth and in French, but only a few. You have to grow up some day. My mom often says, *one of the most basic rules is to show a strong sense of responsibility at a given age, especially when it comes to creating another life.* Creation is not to be taken lightly. Two people who come together begin writing their story à deux. That is a serious matter.

I sure would like to know how I'm going to find out if there are any mistakes in this damn book! It's not like I can wait to be in university to check for myself; my parents will have split up long before that!

I have got to do something. I can't stand by and watch my parents' relationship fall apart.

If my parents do separate they'll end up in court, not that they'll be incarcerated. They'll be acquitted, and I'll be left serving the sentence instead.

I don't want to have to pay their lawyers, although I know that in the long run children are the ones who pay for any break-up. And costs in adult court can run pretty high.

Normally, children are left out of the whole process since everyone knows what they think, and no one wants to have them take the stand. Kids can't pass muster either at court or in school. They have too much trouble concentrating and can only think of one thing, that this is a sentence for life.

My friend Maxime's big brother Simon is in my mom's class at school, and you should see his marks in French. He's failing miserably. His mind's always off in space, thinking about his parents no doubt. Maybe he sees them as planets so distant that gravity doesn't count. On Earth, though, every action carries weight. Probably something to do with the law of physics. His parents have satellites that revolve around them and only meet at the endth degree.

One thing I do know, Maxime and Simon's universe is expanding. Their parents are moving farther and farther apart and will never be together again.

*

Simon knows how to read; maybe he could finish this whole book without falling asleep! He knows all about mistakes so maybe he would be able to pick them out. Simon has been making hundreds of mistakes himself because he doesn't give a damn now that his parents are divorced. He couldn't care less about the French language; his new interest is math. All single-parent offspring are more mathematically-inclined, although subtraction is their weak suit.

Two parents minus one dad equals how many and why?

That type of written equation is relatively difficult for a child to comprehend. The first thing you have to realize is that in subtraction the answer is called the "difference." Luckily, separations are increasingly common – that way affected children don't feel quite so alone.

THE WEAPON

When my dad left my mom and me, I didn't shed a tear, mostly because he just went out for groceries. We always do our shopping on Saturdays.

Incidentally, in the time he's been gone my mom has spent all our money in the shops on St. Denis. The butcher's, the baker's, *the don't touch a thing, do you hear me?* store, the wine merchant's, the bookstore, and the condom store, but my mom doesn't want me to say that, it's not nice. Not to mention a detour to the florist's shop – there at least we didn't spend a cent.

We didn't go to the toy store though. Not today, but we did the other day. They have wicked weapons for sale. It's quite amazing how realistic toys can look nowadays. But my dad doesn't want me buying any firearms, not today, not in our day, not tomorrow, not ever. He made himself quite clear.

It's not normal not to have a rifle when you're a kid. Once I'm grown up, it will be too late. A rifle's too dangerous then.

I do have a rifle made of wood. It's more symbolic than lethal, though. My rifle is a sharp pointed stick with a piece of board nailed on to form the butt and a nail for the trigger. Don't go thinking I could use it to hurt anyone! My mom thinks so and was quick to point that out to my dad. The upshot is that my only means of defence will probably be confiscated from me any day now.

I won't draw a picture of my weapon for you because it's too much like a caricature of itself. It's a joke. The only thing I slay with my piece of wood are my friends, but they all die laughing. At me. All of them, every single one. My friends have real weapons; I would never have thought they could be so cruel.

It's not for want of money that my weapon looks the way it does; we too have a budget for military ends. My weapon looks the way it does because my dad fancies himself a handyman and likes to teach me lessons. I don't like the do-it-yourself look. My friends and their parents all bought prepackaged lessons, most likely from an establishment that hires specialists: soldiers, dictators, pedagogues, babysitters, or sometimes even priests.

I'm the only kid on my street whose dad won't buy her a machine gun.

Generally speaking, my dad can't say no to me although he can say no to my mom. It doesn't bother her one bit, she just goes ahead and does what she wants anyway.

My dad has never had the last word with any of the women in his life, not counting Marie Auger. But she died. It was too good to last.

My dad can't say no to me except when it comes to firearms, candy, and video games.

Anyway, Maxime and all my other friends have machine guns that make all kinds of noise, sparks, and what have you. Sometimes we even play evil space invaders, but how good are my chances of survival without a store-bought weapon and with only my imagination to help me fight off enemies much more dangerously imaginary than me?

The reason all my friends have proper weapons is that they are royal pains who have to defend themselves from the guillotine.

I'm only a princess, and all I have is a piece of wood – a daddy-special – to fight off evil anarchists. How could there possibly be any order in my life?

PAPER

I still haven't introduced myself.

I'm a young bit of a thing, a bean sprout of a girl, what else can I say?

It's a nuisance having only words to describe myself. Words are useless, especially when you consider photography, which does the same thing, only objectively and with precision. But I don't take pictures because I don't have a camera. Now my mom is very well-equipped: she has her own darkroom in the basement. The red light looks pretty bad, but it's not like my mom is a punk or some teenager going through a stage – she needs the light to do her developing, that's all.

My mom takes all the pictures in our family. She won't let me borrow her equipment because she says I'm always breaking things and that all her supplies cost too much; she won't even let me use her special paper to make crafts.

I can't take pictures, but my dad does let me draw on his writing paper.

I'm going to do a sketch of myself for you to make it easier to introduce myself. If a picture's worth a thousand words, just imagine how many pages you save every time you draw just one picture. Seven, three, who knows? In any case, that's how many pages I would have needed to describe myself properly.

Descriptions of princesses are always lengthy. It's a well-known fact that all princesses wear long trains and sometimes crinolines and sequined bustiers studded with alternating black and white pearls; they wear gloves to their elbows; their slippers are often made of glass, and the resulting translucidity becomes the focus of particularly complex descriptions; their crowns showcase thousands of diamonds flashing the whole colour spectrum, and their necklaces likewise, etc. The description can go on for seven or five pages, even more.

So I'll draw a picture of myself. The picture won't take up more than a page, maybe less, which means a savings of at least several pages. And if you multiply those several pages by the number of printed copies of this book, it must add up to tons and tons of paper.

I'm very ecologically minded. As an environmental measure, I would like to suggest that you lend this book to your friends to read or to have their parents read to them so they don't have to buy it themselves. Depending on how old your friends are, help them see all the savings to be made in terms of dollars and cents they can add to their piggybank and use to buy gum with or, when they're older, tranquillizers, if this book doesn't put them to sleep, which I myself would find surprising since it does the job for me.

Don't forget to tell your friends that a good number of copies of this book are on library shelves.

Or, if you're under five, do what I'm doing and wait to start school since this book might be part of the curriculum soon in your future school, either language arts or ethics, and you'll be able to take it out for free.

Any excuse not to buy this book and save our forests is a good one.

Trees are very important. We have to think of conservation; everyone has a role to play, except my dad's publisher. I've met him, since I often tag along with my dad. If he had let me, I would have written in bold on the cover of this book:

REMEMBER! BY BUYING THIS BOOK,
YOU'RE KILLING A TREE!

He nixed the idea.

Books aren't the only things made of paper; money is too, and trees are felled to make more money with. Rich people can't stand the shade trees cast because they want their place in the sun. That's why they all wear dark glasses. People who wear tinted glasses probably have something to hide, like their eyes. I don't like people who are dishonest or greedy. The day they decide to pave St. Louis and put up a parking lot, guess what will be first to go.

THE DRAWING

I still haven't introduced myself.

That's what happens whenever I don't hold my dad's hand. I wander off. I run every which way, especially the wrong ones.

The other day, for instance, I dropped my dad's hand for what couldn't have been more than two minutes and disappeared.

During my escapade, I met a man: the man from the mobile canteen. The canteen is a truck filled with food. It makes as much noise as a firetruck, as though the eradication of famine is an urgent affair.

He's a very nice man, and he offered me some fruit juice. I said no, despite my raging thirst. My thirst is something else. I have a constant burning need to rehydrate. I even wake up at night I'm so thirsty, which is great! I don't know where that nocturnal habit came from, but I'm quite proud of it. Any excuse not to sleep is a good one.[3]

So I turned down his fruit juice.

---

3   Notice to parents of young children: excessive thirst followed by frequent and abundant urination, often nocturnal, is a symptom of diabetes. Author's note.

At my nursery, they told us never to accept sweets from strangers. But does fruit juice qualify as a sweet?

My parents are of two minds on that matter. According to my mom, juice is not really a sweet. My dad, however, is categorical. According to him, *all those junk-food drinks are loaded with sugar!* Rather than come down on one side or the other, I've decided to look at the issue from another angle.

The way I see it, if I'm introduced to someone, then that person is no longer a stranger so I can accept juice from him, regardless of its sugar content.

So I introduced myself to the man from the canteen, just as I'm introducing myself to you.

charlots

That's me.

Of course, you'll notice that's not a halo I'm holding. It's a crown. I don't wear it on my head though because it's too big for me. The other day I tried to put it on my head, and it dropped down onto my shoulders. I made the crown at my nursery during crafts.

As you will note (a fact I have clearly pointed out), I'm not the least bit fat. I was fat when I was little, though. My skin lay in folds. My thighs were all chubby, my hands, arms, and fingers quite pudgy. My cheeks were plump, and I had a double chin. Not that I remember really, but my mom took some great pictures I'd love to show you but won't because I'm not allowed to use the special picture paper.

One day I started to lose weight. The pounds just fell off me, and now I'm as you see me in my sketch.

I'm not fat, right?

Maybe you're thinking that I'm just not very good in art, which is another way of looking at it. It's true that my stick drawings look more like X-rays where not everything that's broken shows up.

If you know how to read, you've also noticed from my drawing that my name is Charlotte.

I wonder why my mom didn't name me after a flower. Daisy, Jacinth, Veronica, Celosia, Violet, Lily, Anemone, or Rose: it's not like she didn't have her pick. Instead she called me Charlotte, the name of a French cake.

I might as well be brutally honest: I'm no piece of cake!

COLOUR

I'm a colourful character.

You can't tell from my drawing, but I have red hair. My eyes are blue, my sweater is red with yellow flowers, my skirt is purple and my shoes are green. It's true, I swear, and not just when I use colourful language. The combinations I choose to mix and match are particularly dreadful. Guess who dressed me this morning?

My dad doesn't want me to use paints or oils when he's writing and I'm sitting at his desk. Which is why the full extent of this fashion disaster is not apparent from my sketch.

Black ink is not a solution for better drawings, it's just a liquid with which to write. One time my dad let me use his feather pen and inkpot.

Once and once only, a decision he bitterly regrets.

I'd barely begun when I managed to knock over the inkpot (I must have been carried away by the heady odour of the black wine) and ruin several paragraphs. All the sentences ran together under the ink, disappearing as they spread across the page in one huge illegible stain.

Oops!

As often happens when I've done something bad, my dad jumps at the opportunity to teach me another lesson.

That's how I learned that you mustn't play with words in an inkpot because of their debility – in other words they're not all there. Their thoughts are so black, they often try to do themselves in. That's why they're shut up like genies in small glass containers. They're crazy, and my dad jabs them frequently with his fountain pen to calm them down.

Which is why it's important never to let them all out of the inkpot at once or you'll end up with a huge fight on your hands like the ones that keep breaking out on schoolgrounds.

Actually, words are also like teenagers. On its own, one word can be just fine, but in a group, words become arrogant and undisciplined. Which makes it harder and harder to make proper sentences, both at school and at home.

Today's youth are only interested in one thing, according to my mom – not working. They certainly never learned that at home since both parents usually work and have done so ever since their children were old enough to walk.

The only thing today's young people want to do is party. They don't want to do French homework. They don't like words, but they do love music. At night, teens retire to their bedrooms to spend hours on the phone. That's why they're called dropouts. In Grade 12, they get together on the phone to organize a grand party. A grand, rad party called grad.

MUSIC

We always speak French at home. "We" means everyone, even Françoise.

Listening to Françoise is like taking a trip abroad. She's from the south of France and *speaks in a singsong,* as my mom says. Françoise is the cleaning woman. I love listening to her; music has a special place in our home.

We always talk French at home.

We discuss punctuation, personal pronouns, auxiliary verbs, verb tenses, etc. Sometimes my mom gets carried away. She thinks my dad makes too many mistakes on his instrument, and she never lets pass an opportunity to settle the score. *You should be practising your conjugation on your own!* To tell the truth, I didn't even know my dad played the conjugation, as a soloist no less.

Poor dad, he doesn't even bother saying a word in his own defence. He knows my mom's right. He's been lax about his work. My mom never metes out any punishment, but you can tell she'd love to rap my dad's knuckles with a rule or two.

As a matter of fact, my grandpa told me that in his day in boarding school little boys were given spankings if they didn't do their homework or do as they were told. Teachers often used their belts as makeshift whips, but the practice has been dying out ever since the prof es sores were caught with their pants down. Some would even whip out their yardstick, which was particularly painful, but with the advent of the metric system, I presume children are no longer subjected to such harsh treatment.

*

If my mom ever saw a mistake in my dad's book, I honestly think it would mean the end of their life together. It goes without saying that my dad needs my help. If not to write, at least to make it come out right. I can't be a silent witness to the canonic attack on his grammatical skills while risking orphalinity with each new maternal invective. One day my dad will have had enough – he'll leave, and not just to go to the grocery store this time. And I'll finish my days abandoned and alone. My dad will be far away, and my mom will be at school.

When French is the subject of discussion at home, nobody notices me. My parents forget my very existence. They let me do as I please. I can burp and fart without so much as an "excuse me," I can ask for milk without saying "please," and I can even use neologisms like "orphalinity" or any old swear word.

But if I really want to interrupt their discussion, I have a whole repertory of colourful words which, strung together, swing their attention to me.

"The deterioration in orthographical competencies of the under 20 age group is a direct consequence of general laxness in the social fabric."

I haven't found a better blasphemy yet. It works every time. Their quarrel ends then and there, as they both turn to ask me to repeat what I just said. Generally, I only manage a partial rendition then quickly change subjects to go on to my own concerns, to things that affect me directly.

THE RACKET

To get back to my earlier story, the man from the canteen didn't kidnap me, and I didn't drink any fruit juice because my dad arrived in time to save me from his clutches.

The man parks his canteen not far from our house because of the street repair gangs working nearby.

Until very recently, there was another gang working the night shift at our neighbours' – an Anglo gang of rockers hot at it, playing boom! boom! boom! bang! bang! bang!, not to mention some worn-out refrains.

They weren't just vocal, they were loud.

All the blaring music kept me awake. I couldn't have asked for more!

Despite his anti-cop bias, my dad – the biggest spoilsport I know – dialed 911. My dad doesn't like the police, but I'll wait for them to show up before I get into that.

The cops didn't come to our house this time (so I'll have to get into that at a future date), they went straight to the musicians' house and proceeded to take away their licence to demolish the neighbours' ears. All the heavy equipment operators had to leave on the spot, thus putting an end to their heavy metal concert.

My dad's not like me, he doesn't like music that cuts into my sleep.

Across from us is a real worksite with real workers renovating a real house. They make as much racket as the group I just told you about, but during the day. They only keep me awake at naptime, which is still better than nothing.

With summer coming it's the same every year, there's always a huge din outside: the revving of motorbikes, portable radios, jack hammers, lawn mowers, and the Italians next door. The latter are extremely noisy, and their conversations and vociferations make for very loud music. The Santinis are our friends. Personally, I like Nino best, he's the youngest in the family. He's always arguing madly, and, with the first rays of sun in spring, you can even watch the way his gestures match his words.

We can see the whole family clearly at mealtimes on their veranda. Their family is something else! There are way too many of them to count. When they all start talking at once, they're like an orchestra suffering from teenage angst.

Once they invited my dad, my mom, and me over for supper.

During the meal, Mr. Santini monopolized the conversation. My dad and mom had a hard time getting a word in edgewise, which meant they had time to chew each mouthful carefully. Mr. Santini didn't speak with his mouth full, but just about.

While the adults conversed and savoured the veal scallopini, pesto pasta, bread, and wine, Nino and I devoured each other with our eyes, like real cannibals, while flashing big grins. We didn't exchange a word. Italians aren't used to silence, which may explain why Mr. Santini's attention suddenly turned to us. Then he pointed and said *sono innamorati!* and my dad said it's *as plain as the nose on your face.* At this, my mom stared hard at me and witnessed the transformation my face had undergone because of the new emotion stirring inside me. She asked *Where did you put your glasses, Charlotte?* My heart made me take them off. I was in love.

My mom does the same for love's sake, she always takes her glasses off to be in love with my dad; he thinks it makes her even more beautiful, and so they are in love together. I too wanted to please Nino even more but, in all honesty, it is only with glasses that one can truly see.

GLASSES

Whether or not you know how to read, you'll have seen from my drawing that I wear glasses.

It's just not fair.

None of the geekiest descriptions of princesses (often included in the most soporific tales) ever mentions a princess who wears glasses. Not a single one!

But I have no choice. It's glasses or nothing. Without them, I can't see a thing.

They say it's a shame.

At least, any grown-up we meet always seems to think it's a shame to see a little girl wearing glasses. That's what they usually say to my parents and me. *What a shame and poor little thing* are the expressions used most frequently, closely followed by *and how old are you, you pretty little thing?*

I don't think it's a shame, except about not eating sweets, that is. I don't really care though and sometimes I go ahead and eat sweets anyway when my parents aren't around – a rare occurrence, so I have a hard time sneaking any without them finding out. My dad always has his eye on me, and you know what he's capable of when I break his stringent food rules. Tell me, is banning sweets any way to treat your child? Personally, I hate Hallowe'en more than any other day of the year. In my section of the nursery, we pretend Hallowe'en doesn't exist because it's the day of the walking dead.

It's a well-known fact that people who give candy to kids like me are out to kill us. And when sugar doesn't do the trick, they resort to hiding razor blades and needles inside the fruit my diet does allow.

Hallowe'en is a day for the walking dead, for evil spirits and ghosts, masked pedophiles and loaded spiders; it's a day for Zorro, Dracula, Batman, and Robin and other transsexuals from Transylvania; it's a day for busy zombies and disinterred heteros; it's a day for cadavers and skeletons in varying stages of decay, a day for wicked witches. A perfect recipe for wicked nightmares once your eyes are shut!

I, however, don't even have to shut my eyes to have nightmares. My imagination is enough. I don't even have to shut my eyes to not see anymore, I just have to take my glasses off my face.

I have serious problems with my eyes.

I have retinopathy, but my dad tries to restrain me. There are words I'm not allowed to use, but they're still in my head along with the strange pictures they evoke.

Based on my dad's description of Hallowe'en, I definitely don't feel much like going out. All the rotting-toothed monsters have killed any craving I might have for candy. I think that's exactly what my dad was hoping for.

THE ILLNESS

I can't read or write.

That's a serious condition, you know.

My dad takes me regularly to see an ophthewallologist. He's a specialist. He checks to see whether his patients can read words oph the wall. Generally speaking, when there's no serious problem, people take the test normally, reading the lines from big to small oph the poster hanging on the wall.

In my case, that's all just a big waste of time.

I don't even try to pass the test. I can't understand a thing on the poster, except a few syllables here and there.

The doctor checks me out using instruments instead. He looks into my eyes and sees into my head. *Just what I was afraid of*, he says to my dad. They don't say anything to me directly because of the severity of my case, but I know anyway. I've known the diagnosis for a long time....

I can't read.

I fully realize just how serious a condition this not reading can be. The consequences of my shortcoming stare me in the face every day. Not being able to read is a tragedy that's especially unforgivable when your mother teaches French and your father writes.

I can't read or write, nor am I making any progress on either score. Don't imagine for a second that my parents are falling all over themselves bribing me with sweets, usually such a welcome treat and an incentive that can't be beat! My parents won't give me sweets under any circumstances. Ever. That's why I'm a diabetic. Not that it's a big deal for anyone other than my dentist.

I've only been to the dentist's once, and I'm never going back. He told me that all my teeth would fall out. Pretty soon I bet I'll look like Lucienne without her false teeth.

Lucienne is my friend. She's also my mom's aunt. I met her in the incinerator – the old folks' home if you prefer. Most people do. Having one's parents at home can be bothersome, I should know. Once life has pretty well burnt them out, they're shipped from the family hearth to the incinerator, where the job is finished off, sometimes even before they're dead.

No wonder the thought of getting old is so distressing.

THE SWEATER

While my dad was doing groceries, my mom and I did all the shops on St. Denis (the butcher's, the baker's, the *don't touch a thing, understand?* store, the wine merchant's, the bookstore, and the condom store, but my mom still doesn't want me to say that; not to mention the florist's which I'll get to shortly), and now we're broke.

We're probably going to have to rob a bank.

Money is important. That's just the way life is, there's not a thing you can do about it even if it's a crying shame. Since I'm way too young to hold down an honest job, I've become somewhat of a thief.

The shoe wasn't my first heist. I stole a chocolate chip cookie from the bakery one day because my dad never buys me any, a baby magazine from the newsstand and, more recently, a childsize bottle of cognac.

My technique is always the same: I just slip the coveted object under my sweater.

I'd never have been caught if the chocolate chips hadn't melted and left incriminating evidence on my stomach and inside my sweater.

My dad gave me a severe talking-to and glaring-at. As I've already mentioned, my dad flips out when it comes to food, especially if it's sweet. When I steal alcohol, though, it's like he can't be bothered to ream me out. He just says *that's not nice* followed by the usual trite reprimands. Go figure.

One day, he's going to have to smarten up or I'll end up in prison. Then who will read me to sleep?

I'm a bit of a kleptomaniac, and my mom isn't happy about that. She probably thinks that my dad is teaching me words that are much too complex for my age.

If I have a chance, I'll tell you about some of my greatest heists.

As I was saying, my mom and I were doing our own shopping and her credit cards were almost chock-a-block, my blue buggy too – with big shopping bags. Now that I can walk for ages without getting tired, my coach has been converted into a shopping cart, often with me pushing from behind.

The reason we bought so many things is that my mom's girlfriends are coming over tonight. I hope they'll have had their babies by now. The last time they came over, I know they were both pregnant. They'd hidden the babies in their stomach, but the cache was too large not to be seen.

I was pregnant just the other day. My belly was huge. I'd hidden a small doll under my sweater, just like my mom's friends.

I talked to my baby and told her a story every night. That's a must. We all have an inner child we must talk to. Of course, boys don't understand that. Only pregnant girls know what's what.

I had my baby by cesarean – minus the shots, naturally – and I didn't scream, unlike my mom. Did she ever yelp when she caught sight of me! I'd cut the front of my nice red sweater to let my baby out, and my mom was really mad.

Hearing her yelp, my dad stepped in and slapped her across the face. She fell to the ground, and he finished the job with a few swift kicks to her ribs. But my mom wasn't dead. She stood up when his back was turned, grabbed the scissors lying on the floor, and drove them between his shoulder blades. My dad crumpled to his knees, then to his stomach on the floor.

I should say right now before you start to dial 911 that the last paragraph did not take place in my family, but a similar scene really did occur in a movie I saw at Maxime's house, without a word of a lie. My parents won't hear tell of me watching that kind of movie. They say it might put ideas into my head.

IDEAS

We often go to the florist's, but just to browse.

Or that's what we say…

Actually, we're there to steal. With my mom, stealing's okay. In fact, she encourages it when she's with me.

We never buy flowers at the florist's because we have hundreds of flowers at home. We abscond with something else, without exchanging a word in advance so as not to get caught.

My mom gives me the sign, pointing discreetly to a superb hibiscus in bloom. Growing at its base are several young shoots of *chlorophytum* and *hypoestes*. They're all planted together in a big clay pot with an Egyptian or Indian design, I'm not sure which. All I know is it's gorgeous. The whole arrangement is priced at *three hundred dollars! That's highway robbery!* exclaims my mom. And we make our getaway. Sight unseen.

My mom and I steal nothing but ideas. Our purpose in going to the florist's is to breathe in the scents. We scout out the possibilities and look for inspiration in the floral arrangements there.

They are magnificent. Just the sight of all the plants that don't grow here, I mean outdoors, makes our mouth water. We do have several indoor plants, but not quite as many as outdoors. The outdoor plants don't have as many flowers so we often choose them for their distinctive leaves.

Everyone loves the flower best, because it's a plant's sexual organ. That's why you have to watch out for sexual predators. My mom warned me. Insect and incest do not mean the same thing. Both feed on flowers, but one is treated with pesticides and the other with parricides. Although chemical extermination is harmful to the environment, it's highly effective. You mustn't be afraid to resort to it. Flowers are so beautiful, so fragile, they must be protected at all costs.

And to think that my dad actually eats them!

*

From the florist's we went to the shoeist's. That's when I discovered we were bankrupt. Believe it or not, we went to a store in which every shoe had already been worn by other women who'd left their names inside; Nina Ricci was one of them. She had an entire collection!

My mom was obviously broke.

That's when I had the brilliant idea of taking a shoe from the display case. I slipped it under my sweater on the sly. I know, it was only one shoe, but the following week they'd have to take the other shoe out of its box and put it on display.

The hardest part would be convincing my mom to go back. Or at least that's what I thought at the time. As you'll see, it turned out that not only did I not have to convince her, I was forced, first by her and then by my dad, to go back to that damn shoe-ster's.

THE SCENE

My mom knows nothing about my theft. The shoe makes a bulge under my sweater, but she hasn't noticed a thing yet. How can I announce my newest offence?

I don't dare spring it on her right away. Deep down, I know she's not going to be very happy. She's going to make a scene. If I show her the spoils of my misdemeanour, she'll call the cops for sure and I'll end up in prison, surrounded by thieves, rapists, and other scum who'll not stop at anything anywhere.

What story can I tell and still be free?

We were unpacking our purchases on the table. My mom was taking hers out of the bags when I suddenly gave birth to a shoe, without tearing my sweater this time. As I'd suspected, my mom was not happy. It showed in her mournful vowels. *Chaaarlooootte, where did you get that shoe?*

I told her the truth.

As it turned out, she didn't call the police.

My mom was not at all happy. I should have clued in beforehand: my mom doesn't like red shoes. They're the kind only a slut would wear.

My mom doesn't like to hear me say "slut." She says it's vulgar, crude and dirty coming from a young girl's mouth. Françoise calls me *cochonne* sometimes – little Ms. Piggy – because of my filthy talk! I find that "slut" just kind of trips off my tongue; it's short and to the point, but what can I say? It was not a good time to argue.

Instead of taking me to the police, my mom marched me back to the store to return the shoe.

I told you she would make me take it back.

We had to hurry because the store closes at six o'clock. But since I can't read a clock or a book, I dragged my feet the whole way there; we ended up having to run. We had to run across St. Denis because the store was going to close any minute. That's when I dropped the shoe smack in the middle of the road. I managed to free my hand from my mom's grasp and run back to pick it up. Just as I bent over, I saw a car heading straight for me. My mom saw it too and sort of panicked, probably because a side trip to what Françoise calls the *cleeneeque* was not part of her plan. My appointment wasn't until Monday. My mom certainly has a good pair of lungs on her, better than I thought. Her scream drowned out the half dozen tires screeching as though in common accord. To avoid hitting me, the first car ran into the car beside it which hit a third car parked on the street.

It was quite the pileup, like a rad movie, one with lots of violence, the kind my dad won't let me watch so I save them for Maxime's house, not this weekend though.

As soon as enough people were on the scene, the police appeared like a shot.

The police…

I was scared shitless that my mom would turn me in. Scared shitless is not a nice expression either. Luckily, I think my mom had forgotten all about it – the shoe I mean – and there was no way I was going to stick 'em up. I kept both hands behind my back, a firm grip on the shoe.

The ambulance was next on the scene, to pick up the driver of one of the cars. I owe that man my life. I hope he'd already booked an appointment at Emergency, otherwise he could be in for a long wait. I know all about hospitals, I have one of my own. But I'll get back to that later since I have a number of appointments coming up.

My mom just about got hit too, but that's because she fainted in one of the lanes.

Everyone forgot about me. I would have thought someone would have signed me up on the spot for the closest kindergarten now that the Governor General's government is handing out subsidies. That's not what happened.

A man abducted me.

I would have been a major traffic hindrance if I'd stayed put on the street. A man kindly held out his hand, but I don't think he was a pedophile because he didn't offer me candy. He was just a good Samaritan. He kept holding his hand out to me, but I didn't budge. There was no way I was going to let him see my shoe. Since I insisted on keeping my hands behind my back, he gathered me up in his arms, just about knocking me over in the process. I had to swing my arms out and grab onto his neck whereby I let go of the shoe without thinking. It went flying into the crowd and hit someone square in the eye, high heel first, or at least that's the way it seemed. In any case, there was blood.

I was in for it now. I'd probably be charged with assault resulting in injury, criminal negligence, obstruction of justice, attempted murder, robbery, hit-and-run, and who knows what else.

Finally, the good Samaritan turned me in to the police, who handed me over to my mother lying on a stretcher. She was going to be all right. Together the two of us left, but not in the direction of the shoe store. With all the goings-on, the store had closed ages ago and wouldn't re-open until Monday. I knew I'd be coming back with my dad. There was no getting out of it.

At least I'd been given a reprieve.

*

We went back home, mission unaccomplished, but at least we rode in a police car. The whole way there I was afraid my mom would mention my shoplifting offence, but luckily she was still in shock.

The cops had quite the piece in their squad car. No way could I ignore that! I even asked if it was an automatic weapon and if I could pull the trigger, just once, a reasonable request. They turned me down.

I pouted all the way home.

Pouting usually works every time, but those mean-spirited cops didn't change their mind.

Police or no, my dad decided to let them in. He doesn't like policemen because of the bad cops in their midst; you can't tell the good from the bad though because they all wear the same uniform. My dad must have seen my mom and me standing behind the cops to have opened the door. He knew we were on our way because of a stoolpigeon in our midst. People sometimes call stoolpigeons Judases, but my dad doesn't like anything to do with the Bible either. There are all kinds of things and people my dad hates, except my mom, her friends, and me.

Luckily, the officers didn't get on anyone's case. They just dropped us off and left.

Because of all the excitement the meal wasn't ready when my mom's girlfriends turned up a short while later. My dad ordered in pizza for everyone, even me.

My mom's friends were more pregnant than ever, and my dad served them a glass of white. My dad would never let a pregnant mother have a glass of red in our house. White or nothing. My dad flips out when it comes to food. So my mom's friends and I drank milk. Does it ever taste gross with pizza! My dad and mom sipped on wine.

Seeing my mom's pregnant friends made me feel kind of lonely. I would so like to see friends more often. I think my dad noticed.

Often when I feel sad I'm allowed to drown my sorrows in fresh grape juice served in a breakable cup. Sometimes my dad tries to fool me and uses plastic cups that look exactly like the glass ones. I dropped my cup on purpose to see whether he'd tried to pull one over on me again. He hadn't, not this time, and there were shards of broken glass everywhere. Whenever I break a glass, they make me pick up the pieces. I always have to pick up after myself. It's part of my upbringing. I always manage to cut myself on the glass, and blood stains pretty badly, just as much as grape juice. My dad got angry because I smeared red all over my clothes; I can't find words to describe how furious he got. I went to bed under equally indescribable conditions. I bought it big time. There was slapping, kicking, punching, and then the coup de grâce, the reading of a tale whose ending I'll never know since by that time I'd passed out.

THE KITE

Long before sailors began crisscrossing the ocean, a tender-hearted giant named Sylvester lived on a small island cut off from the rest of the world. He grew to such a remarkable giant size because of his son's death. After the tragic loss of his son, Sylvester sought refuge in the forbidden forest where he ate thousands of berries from what was said to be a deadly bush. Instead of losing his life though, he grew and grew and grew.

Every day thereafter, the only place Sylvester could find solace was in the laughter of the children whose kites he untangled from the branches of thousand-year-old trees. The rest of the time he lived alone, feared by all.

Now one day, as the big-hearted Sylvester drew near the park, he wasn't greeted by the usual loud laughter. The children were no longer there.

As he turned back toward home, sad and lost in thought, he spied on a rooftop the Island Dreamer, a tiny man, making kites.

"Giant," shouted the Dreamer to make sure he made himself heard, "all the island children have stopped laughing and playing! Late yesterday I was testing my new kite when it brushed up against a huge black cloud. A strange drizzle began to fall and silenced the little ones.

Wise Cornelius says that someone must make his way to the continent on the far east side of the world to gather up one of the first rays of the rising sun for order to be restored. The only person capable of crossing the ocean without drowning is you."

Without a word, Sylvester returned home in two huge strides to gather up a few provisions and a little heart-shaped box, then set off immediately, the faraway echo of children's laughter ringing in his ears....

THE MORNING

I slept like a log, wouldn't you know it!
I didn't wake up once through the night. If I did
have nightmares, I don't remember them, I wasn't
dying of thirst and I didn't pee my bed. I slept like
a log, thus ruining another night. Sleep is time lost
– it's death by management. I want to waste time. I don't want to budget for
sleep. I can't wait to have a programmed alarm
clock like my mom has, one that works better than
my biological clock, which skips a few beats every
night. Better still, I dream of having my own children who'll cut into my sleep a dozen times a night,
hash it up fine. A thousand times better yet would
be to have a newborn to crack open my sleep like an
egg and beat my nights until they're thoroughly
whipped.

*

Fortunately, thanks to our big Sunday brunch I'm
reconciled to life. Hardboiled eggs, scrambled eggs,
butter croissants, buttered toast, English muffins,
French cheese, pâté, ham, bacon – the works.

Everyone samples a bit of everything, everyone except me that is. I have to pass on maple syrup and jam. I'm given cinnamon-flavoured whipped cream instead. I put a ton of cream on all the fruit: blueberries, raspberries, strawberries, cantaloupe, green grapes, clementines, and that star-shaped thing. To think that all this wonderful fruit used to be beautiful flowers. Flowers taste so good when they're juicy, you just have to be patient.

My dad doesn't always wait long enough; he's too impatient. He's even teaching me to be impatient. You should never wait. Patience is a virtue for those who don't realize how desperately short life is. You have to hurry or else you'll miss out, and life will pass you by like a scent on the breeze.

That's why I insist on staying awake as late as possible. My dad can be quite contradictory; he's against my objection to sleep. We're two of a kind, both strong willed; we don't pull any punches when it comes to bedtime. Evenings are the chosen ground for all the fights and stories my dad and I engage in. I don't want to sleep and I show it, and then my dad claims I'm acting up.

Acting up, me?!!!

Now if that doesn't beat all!

And the characters in my bedtime stories, what about them? All their interminable quarrels that are interrupted in the most horrific way!? Hard-hitting tales wherein I'm deprived of the coup de grâce, captivating reads that keep me prisoner in a place where no holds are barred, where words rain down in an unrelenting effort to beat me back to the land of nod! The torture goes on and on. The next day my dad starts back at the beginning, never where I nodded off. There can be no suffering greater than knowing it will never end.

FEAR

My dad is on the wanted list with the Youth Protection Branch.

But today I'm the one in hiding. I'm in my dad's green bedroom under his bed, and I have the phone from his night table by my side, just in case. I lie still and don't make a sound so no one will find me. I'm scared. My dad has even grown a beard. He's unrecognizable. He looks like Bluebeard only his is black. He really scares me.

He's downstairs looking for me.

He wants to kill me. That's why I dialled 911, but I couldn't speak when the lady answered because my dad would have heard me as soon as I opened my mouth so I hung up.

He really scared me with his disguise. It looked disturbingly real. But we were just play-acting. He was the mean pirate and I was the good siren, but not for real. And I don't mean a siren like the one on the police car that jerked to a halt in front of our house.

My dad had his sword in hand when the police burst into the house. His long sabre is a souvenir from a trip. He uses it to open bottles of champagne.

I'm always allowed a sip, but only one because champagne has quite a kick. You try explaining that particular use for a sabre to a cop who drinks his beer straight from the bottle and his wine from a cardboard box! I know, I know, I sound prejudiced, but when prejudice is entertained, it can last and last.

My dad even tried to explain why he was carrying a weapon; he said we were acting out a fairy tale and it was just make-believe; once again you try explaining the basics of stage direction to a cop who's never been to the theatre and whose only reading material has been the Criminal Code!

My dad wasn't wearing any accessories other than his days-old beard and his sharp sabre. My costume, on the other hand, was quite elaborate so he pointed to me by way of explanation.

I was wearing a blond wig and a green garbage bag cinched with a belt at the waist to make me look like a real mermaid with a smooth fish tail. I had to hop like a sea lion to move around.

When Mr. Police Officer asked me if we were really just playing make-believe, I corroborated our scenario by saying, "He wants to kill me."

My dad glared at me, which only made matters worse.

My guess is that the police thought the lower portion of my body hidden inside the green bag had already been hacked to bits. The next thing they knew I'd be abandoned in a ditch somewhere along a country road or dumped into a river tied to a block of cement for ballast.

My mom wasn't home right then or else I'm sure she could have straightened the police out with tact and diplomacy. But she had gone to church. Normally I go with her, but since she would be at home the next day because of the holidays and since we'd be spending a lot of time together starting tomorrow, I didn't. Of course, my mom doesn't believe in religion. She goes to church almost every Sunday for the free concerts, that's all.

We managed to sweet-talk our way out of it by ourselves.

Luckily, my dad wasn't served a summons because the only advocate we have is the one we managed to grow once. Now that was a great horticultural activity! We took three pits (we'd just made a shrimp-advocate salad), stuck in toothpicks and put them in a glass full of water so that the bottom part of each pit was in contact with the nourishing liquid. Only one advocate germinated, but it's grown into a thriving plant.

Anyhow, my dad was lucky and the officers let him off with a warning.

THE TRUTH

It's not true about my dad. I mean about all the slapping, punching, and kicking. He's never hit me with his fists; he hasn't even offered me a hit. My dad bashes smoking not his kid.

My dad's not like that, and I'm like him. I have a great imagination. That's what happens when people read you all kinds of stories and tales. You say things that boggle the mind.

While I'm on the subject, I should also admit that I've never picked up pieces of glass with my bare hands either. But it is true that whenever I drop real grape juice, oil paints, potatoes, etc. on the floor, I take the rap, even though we have Françoise. On the other hand, the 911 and Bluebeard story is true.

Françoise does the dishes and cleans our house. My dad hates housework too much. I'm no Cinderella and neither is my dad – he's not the kind to wash floors and keep his mouth shut.

Françoise looks after all that now. My dad used to before my mom hired Françoise, but he always did a half-assed job. That's another word you shouldn't use, instead you should say half-hearted.

That's why my mom hired Françoise, because she uses proper French. Besides, Françoise is old and ugly. My mom picked her on purpose because my dad is young and handsome, and my mom wants the job done right. My dad and I have a nickname for Françoise – Franchovy – it's always good for a laugh! The nickname's dumb, and Françoise doesn't find it funny. That's what makes us laugh. All this may sound childish, but once my dad and I are grown up the time for kidding around will be past.

*

I'm big on eating. When I was little, I used to fan my food out in a one-metre radius around my high-chair. I'm a difficult child. I'm not like other people, I won't eat just anything. My dad did the initial screening of my food, then I did the real weeding out, a much more exhaustive process. I got hold of any undesirables with both hands and threw them out of sight whether my dad agreed or not. Unfortunately, my dad often got caught in the middle, which left the offending food group in view still, right under my nose. Actually, under my dad's nose since it was caught in his beard. Luckily, a mashed-potato face has never really bothered him.

I've calmed down somewhat over the years – now I eat with a catapult. I also have a carrot launcher that would make a great rocket launcher, but I don't use my arsenal anymore to attack imaginary enemy strongholds.

My dad is always home so he's the one who makes our meals. My meals are another story. My dad flips out over food. With my mom it's flowers, with my dad it's grub. Some day we're going to have a huge vegetable garden. I don't eat just anything, except for vegetables and fruit which have all been okayed. Everything else has to be measured out. My dad's been extra careful ever since I ended up in Intensive Care. In a coma. That was some experience! A diabetic coma. That same day we learned I have diabetes and I had my first shot, but I was already asleep. Ever since, whenever I feel the least bit sleepy, I'm afraid I'll never wake up. I know too well just how deep sleep can be.

THE PUZZLE

I'm a worry to my parents on several counts. Out of concern for me, they've made decisions that have totally changed the course of my existence.

Everything that happens to me leaves its mark. Because of the life I've led, I'm different from other kids my age. I have marks on my stomach, my thighs, and my arms, but they're nothing compared to the rest. As for the shots, maybe I'll get used to them some day.

I'm not quite normal.

I'm not like other kids of the VCR generation whose parents could do with an IUV. My parents don't suffer from exhaustion, except my mom when she comes back from teaching school every day. She has trouble keeping on top of things because teenagers are so big. So my dad's the one who sees to my upbringing, another source of worry for my mom.

As incredible as this may sound, my dad taught me almost everything I know. I realize how abnormal that is. Generally speaking, that's a babysitter's job or sometimes a mom's.

I love having a writer for a dad. Writers don't work, and they're always at home. They live in their own little world, and in my dad's kingdom there's a huge domain reserved for me.

My dad loves me so much that I can make him be or do anything I want. And I mean anything: a horse, a plane, a bear, a puppy dog, a bug, or a writer of big-lettered books, not an easy task even for a novelist.

Novel writing is tough because every time my dad sits down at his desk to write his story, his big story, I get in the way. I sweep all the paper off the desk and set up my twenty-four-piece puzzle, and a look of discouragement crosses his face. No wonder, twenty-four pieces is a lot!

He gives up on work then and helps me with my puzzle. It can take hours. Sometimes his gaze wanders back to the computer screen, but I grab his prickly chin every time and turn his face back to me. Holding up a piece of the puzzle, I say, "Daddy! Daddy! Does this one go here?"

Uh-huh, little princess, he says distractedly.

But I've taken the wrong one on purpose.

"No, Daddy, look. It doesn't fit."

Then he has no choice but to focus all his attention on the task at hand. Often I ask him to tell me a story about the picture my puzzle makes. The hours just fly by... the best hours on Earth.

MY DAD AND ME

My dad and I are very close. We never leave each other's side. We're joined like two fingers, the nose-picking ones. He's the index finger, and I'm the thumb because I'm not as big as he is.

My dad never tells me not to pick my nose. My dad is awesome! He does so many things with me that normal parents wouldn't do. My dad even taught me when to say "Jesus Christ." There's no way my mom would have taught me that because she never uses the expression. When she gets mad, my mom says "damn" or "hell" instead.

My education is something else! Education is important, and my dad doesn't want me getting it in the kindergarten down the street. He doesn't even let me watch movies from Walt Disney Home Videos or any other kind of animated babysitter. Not that I don't have any videos. I have one in particular that I know you'd like to see.

In the video, you can see my parents sitting at the foot of a palm tree. Later on, they're walking hand in hand beneath snow-covered pine trees. As I've already mentioned, before I came along my parents lived a truly fairy-tale existence. They travelled the world, vacationed at the cottage any time they felt like it, and sometimes did things in the kitchen that had nothing to do with preparing meals.

The kitchen sequence in which my dad's hands and my mom's breasts are clearly visible is quite far into the video; often I just about fall asleep before it comes on.

I won't go into my parents' perilous antics as shown in that video because teenagers reading my account might try to imitate them.

You may wonder how it is that I came to be in possession of pornographic material.

Actually, it was quite a fluke….

I thought the tape was the Captain Hook movie my dad pirated off TV. The two video cases look exactly alike except for the sticker with the name of the title, but I don't know how to read, except little words like wawa, daddy, pee, poo, and Nina Ricci. Since my dad balks at any mention of the kindergarten down the street, there's not much hope he'll be in favour of me going to grade school either!

EDUCATION

Education is a must for a princess – an education in good manners, current affairs, arms drills, and the like. My dad teaches me almost everything I know. I say "almost" because you can learn a lot from movies, too.

Personally, I like movies about pirates, princesses, knights, and queens.

Besides *Hook* I really like another video, even though it belongs to my dad and mom, called *Queen Margot*. I always have horrific nightmares whenever I've watched it on the sly, but that's fine by me since I hate to sleep.

My mom claims my dad should never have taught me how to use the VCR. But I learned on my own it was such a snap.

However, when my dad watches TV with me I can't watch what I want. Too many shows are off limits, and he won't even tell me why.

You have to learn to take orders before you're fit to command.

That's a classic dad-ism. He's quite the one for giving orders.

My dad's been trotting out that same old line

ever since I made the mistake of telling him what I wanted to be when I grow up.

It's normal for a princess to want to be a queen. At first, I wanted to be the Governor General and run the whole country, but one has to be reasonable so I decided to start on the bottom rung as a dictator in school. It's all well and good to reign over Carré St. Louis, its snack bar, its public benches, its trees and its flowers, but it can get kind of boring after a while.

I think it would be a lot more exciting to rule a school. Going by what my mom says, there'd be all kinds of action!

In my school, I'd let kids talk all the time in language arts class about their lives at home, on the street, in the schoolyard, all the stuff that really counts. I'd throw in a bit of grammar and spelling every once in a while, but a good teacher should give lots of examples from personal experience because that's what kids are interested in. Children need role models not rule models.

I think children need to have their parents around more than they need a full-time babysitter.

Personally, I've never set foot in a kindergarten so I know what I'm talking about. My parents look after me, not every child can say as much.

I sure hope my dad and mom won't let someone else teach me how to read. That would be too much! They've taught me everything else, haven't they, so why leave the difficult task of literacy training in the hands of strangers? My dad can't abandon me now in my hour of need!

"Father, why have you forsaken me?"

If he does abandon me, that's exactly what I'll say. That will get him. He'll feel guilty and think he's failed in my education.

Most of all, he'll wonder how I came to know the words made famous by Jesus of Nazareth. Actually, I stole them off TV and a movie called, you guessed it, *Jesus of Nazareth*.

It's a good movie with a great message of love, but there's some arm-twisting at the end that's a bit much.

EXISTENCE

My dad and I are as one. You mustn't forget that until I learn to write, free of mistakes no less, I'm under his super vision. All my decisions are made by him. My dad is part of everything I do. When I start playing with pots and pans, he appears; I can't break my milk glass without him having me pick up the pieces on the spot. He's forever on my case, always on my back. He can't live without me anymore. We are as one. My dad joins in all my games, he's lost without me, he always wants me by his side, he has no time left to write, creation has lost all meaning, his autonomy has gone by the wayside, I'm the first one affected, and our lives are screwed.

His life is no longer possible without me, and I think the same holds true for me. If my dad weren't here, maybe I wouldn't exist.

Could I be the product of his imagination?

No way!

I exist. If not, what would happen to the world? The universe needs millions of universes to exist fully, and mine is just as important as the next.

Besides, I'm drawn to a certain future, clear proof of my existence. I know, you think where drawing's concerned my perspective's off and that I should go into Fine Arts, but that's not my plan.[4] I want to study the art of letters, learn how to write and become a writer like my dad. I want to reinvent the world in the naive hope of creating a better one.

---

4   There seems to be some confusion over the meaning of "drawn" at the beginning of the paragraph. Correctrix's note.

CREATION

My dad makes up stories. They're a good write and a great read.

My dad is the strongest, the handsomest, the biggest, and the nicest dad of all, so why wouldn't he be the best novelist too? Actually, every book he's written has been decorated so far. With a price and a GST. There's also a special prize called the Governor General's a ward, so called because each winner becomes a ward to the head of the government's desire to foster literature. My dad says he could do without. He doesn't need GSTs or a wards to write. He'd rather have no special mention at all since books are expensive enough as it is. That's why he writes them himself.

My dad does everything himself. He built the furniture in our house, the house next to the garage, the garage in which he fixes the car, the car we drive to go to the cottage, the cottage he built next to the lake God made.

Whenever I mention Creation, it makes my dad see red. It makes him bloody cross!

My dad told me that God the Father hosts a bash every Sunday at a litigious ceremony during which furious disciples gang up on the host and eat him in the round. That's what we call the Eucharist.

But you have to be careful not to mention God in my dad's presence; he gets beside himself. Anything to do with the Bible gets a rise out of him. The Bible is the most widely sold book in the world, and my dad is horribly jealous. The book is one of the great masterpieces in the fantasy genre, and my dad himself is busy writing a fantastic book inspired by one of the chapters from that hefty tome, the one on Noah's ark.

*

I too want to learn to write, that's what I told my dad. Since he's never going to agree to send me to school, in a magnanimous gesture one day he brought out his bible.

Naturally, my dad's purpose was not to give me a lesson in religion, he wanted to teach me ethics instead: his bible is the authoritative book on the French language entitled *Le bon usage*. He said I would find clear explanations of right and wrong inside and that by practising the three thousand commandments therein, I would be assured of admission through the pearly GATES[5] one day.

---

5   GATES - Great Authors and Terrific Essayists School. Author's note.

GOD, MY FATHER, AND ME

My parents never married and I'm not batized.[6]

Religion can give meaning to life, I know. My dad explained it all to me: the Immaculate Conception, reincarnation, the ban on eating pork, the ingenious ban on transfusions (just imagine, a life without shots!), the sacred cows, the archbishop and his sacraments, and the Eucharist of course, but my dad and I don't indulge.

We don't like eating in the round.

My parents never go to church, except for concerts. Whenever I attend, I fall asleep. Art does it to me every time. I sleepwalk through museums and succumb to the deathly quiet of library halls. Dark theatres and comfortable seats soon get the better of my genuine interest in the fiction and the action on stage.

The other day, my dad took it upon himself to talk to me about the inexistence of God. He wanted to tell me himself before anyone else got to me first. He covered all the bases.

---

6   This is not a misprint; the author categorically refuses to add a p, seeing it as a papal mark. Nasty paranoiac! Correctrix's note.

His explanation followed closely on a bizarre revelation made to me by my cousin Olivier. Olivier told me that Grandpa Théberge is in heaven. I immediately lifted my gaze to the clouds. My cousin did no such thing. I didn't pursue the issue, not wanting to look more stupid and nearsighted than I am, but later I did touch on the matter with my dad.

"Daddy, my eyes must be getting worse again because Olivier said that Grandpa Théberge is in the sky, but I couldn't see him. I must need a stronger prescription for my glasses."

My dad didn't want to book an appointment for me with the ophthewallogist, but we did have a little tête à tête. He explained that my not seeing had nothing to do with my eyes.

I'm not sure I quite understood because it seems so obvious that there's nothing else up in the sky but sun, clouds, birds, and planes, all of which I can see just fine.

My dad took me to a cemetery to help me understand.

I'd never seen a cemetery before. It's like the best park ever because there are all kinds of flowers everywhere! Too many to count.

My mom came along, but she cried the whole time. I couldn't see why: given the number and variety of flowering plants waiting to be identified, we could have indulged in our favourite pastime forever. Who knows, maybe she was feeling unhealthy pangs of jealousy at the sight of so many gorgeous cut flowers.

My dad, however, displayed a new-found interest in geology. The stones were what interested him the most. There were a lot of stones too, but one in particular held his attention. In fact, he made me look at it up close. Always eager to read to me, my dad said that Grandpa's name was written on the stone, but since I can't read that didn't mean much. Then he announced, quite nonchalantly, that Grandpa Théberge was buried underneath. "Jesus Christ, Daddy, we have to do something quick!" I interrupted him.

He wouldn't hear of it. He wouldn't let me dig Grandpa up because he said we didn't have a shovel, which was true.

I don't understand any better now than before. My dad claims that Grandpa's in the ground, and Olivier says he's in the sky.

Who should I believe?

*

My parents have a friend who believes in God, but not for long. There's no way the friendship can last. She and my parents are always having heated exchanges, and I mean real ones. Her name is Claudine. Claudine claims that *even if you don't believe in God, He's inside each and every one of us.* To my astonishment, my dad agreed wholeheartedly, saying: *You're right. In my case, I have had him up to here!*

COLOURFUL LANGUAGE

My dad wanted to write a book with big colourful language just for me. Grandpa and Grandma have trouble seeing too, but they're not diabetic. They're Catholic, nothing too serious, it just pains them to hear me say "Jesus Christ." Every time, my grandma gives a little start. Instead of scolding me, though, she yells at my dad. Awesome, isn't it?

When words in a book are big and colourful, the normal inclination is to think it's a kid's book, but it could be for old folks instead. They're usually the ones who get so frustrated trying to decipher the small print they'd like to tear their eyes out.

It's really gross watching someone have their eyes torn out, let me tell you! I know because I've seen it happen in two movies already. Once was at Maxime's house in *The Night of the Living Dead* during an impromptu vivisection carried out by patients waiting for heart-lung-brain transplants. The operation was clearly meant to be filmed because there were tons of close-ups from every possible angle. The second time was when my mom and I went to see *Jesus of Montreal*. That time actual surgeons performed the operation in a room screened from probing eyes, which made the scene more bearable.

CHARACTER SIZE

I'm small fry.

But I smell good.

Wherever I go, I leave behind an odoriferous wake. That sounds funny. My mom taught me that word. I love to say "odoriferous." All it really means is fragrant, but it's so much more beauticious.

I smell like *Lavandula latifolia*. That's the soap I use, an odoriferous one. My dad likes to gather nectar from my neckbud, and sometimes he almost eats me up. He sinks his teeth into my carotid artery à la *Dada Dracula* for a laugh. It works because he tickles me.

I make him pay, however, for those stolen moments of happiness. I'm no treat, you know. I've often made his life miserable with diapers to change, baths to give, meals to make, puzzles to do, and messes to clean, not to mention all the other chores he delegates to Françoise.

I'm small fry, but my dad's the big cheese.

Sometimes, he abuses his authority.

For instance, when my language is too colourful for his liking, he washes my mouth out with lavender soap. It smells good, but boy does it taste gross. At times I'm consumed by hatred. For my dad, not the soap! What an awful way to treat a child! But I can't speak so I keep my mouth shut. I never thought this was what proper hygiene meant.

When I tell my mom that my dad makes me eat soap – well, almost – you can bet she'll want to kill him again. Bodily cleanliness is important, but you mustn't forget about mental hygiene. Washing a child's mouth out with soap for swearing is something they did in the old days, not anymore.

*

If I keep telling such big whoppers, my dad really will be in trouble with the Youth Protection Branch or, even worse, with the police. He won't be issued a warning next time, he'll be served with a *subpoena*.

By the way, that's not a flower….

THE FLOWER

I love my mom. She's a flower just like me. She smells like spring. My mom is beautiful; she looks very young. Whenever people ask *how old are you, you sweet young thing?* she always says *I have a pretty posy of years to my credit.* And if they insist, asking for the name of the latest flower in her bouquet, she simply says *the primrose of life.* I can't describe that new flower to you because I myself have never seen one, but my mom's skin is imbued with its scent. I could pick it out in any garden anywhere.

I think I'll draw you a picture of my mother so that you can see just how pretty she is.

There, that's my mom.

You can't tell from my drawing, but she has blue eyes and almost red hair and her skin is pure white. Her dress is blue too, but my dad still won't let me use my paint set when I'm in his office with him.

There's no denying we're related. We look a lot alike, except for our hair. My mom's hair is very fine, cut short and straight, not curly like mine, but I always draw my mom as though she were a flower, I'm not quite sure which one, maybe a tulip. In any case it's a sign of love.

That's not me she's holding – it must be a baby in the bud.

I do think my mom is considering having another flower, but not a Passion flower like me. My mom told me all about where I come from, and I wouldn't be surprised to hear that she'd swallowed another seed to have it grow in her belly.

I actually do know how I was conceived. There's even a word for it, but, surprising as it may seem, I can't remember the word. It will probably come back to me later on. I heard the word for the first time one evening when my parents' friends were over. They all probably thought I was sound asleep since they'd read *Little Red Riding Hood* to me. Instead, I woke up in the middle of the night with a nightmare. What else did they expect? A big bad wolf was devouring all the flowers in our garden. I woke up to hear them talking about children and having babies, until they gradually got onto the subject of… I still can't remember the word.

AGE

I never let on how old I am to anyone. I'm like my mom that way.

My mom hasn't told anyone her age since the numbers started moving too fast for her. Nobody ever believed her anyway, unless I was standing nearby as living proof.

But I'm not really all that old. Of course, on the pages of a book I look older than I really am. You're even older still when you start to see the writing on the wall.

I never say how old I am even when I'm asked nicely. But for you, I'll make an exception. I'll tell you if you promise to read the next sentence out loud:

How old are you, sweetheart?

I bet you didn't read it out loud.

I bet you're all in high school. My mom told me that teens never want to join in any activities the teacher organizes to liven up the class. Teens aren't the only ones though. I bet no adults read the sentence out loud either; basically, people just don't like to read.

Maybe you do though. Let me guess, you're reading this book on a bench in Carré St. Louis on a fine summer day. If that's so, I can understand why you didn't read the sentence out loud since everyone around you would have thought you'd gone mad. But I think that's highly unlikely. I bet you're not sitting in my park at all. This book is more the kind you read at night after a hard day's work once the children are finally in bed. But every night, it's the same old story, the children don't want to go to bed so you have to argue, negotiate, promise, threaten, and when you finally manage to tuck them in after having read them some nasty business to do with Prince Charming, you're pooped and you decide to lie down straightaway, at which point, I ask you, do you really feel like reading this kind of book?!?

A TASTE FOR READING

My mom is a teacher, but she refuses to teach me to read and write. She'll teach total strangers, but she won't teach me.

I can't stand it.

My mom is a teacher, and she often talks about school at home. I know all about language arts class. Teens don't listen, they don't like to write, and they don't like to read. That's not surprising given that the teachers my mom works with make their students read books my dad himself would never have dared write for young adults. I won't name any names, or authors or teachers, but there are books that should be reserved strictly for people in search of a cure for insomnia. My mom says that before you can learn to write palatably, you have to have a taste for reading. Otherwise, there's no point.

Now, though, almost all my mom's students love to read and hardly anyone falls asleep in class. That took some doing.

To give them a taste for reading, my mom started each new school year with the same book. The book's opening line is: *If there's one thing in life I can't stand, it's my mother*. You can bet teens want to read after that! They totally identify, and they're hooked!

However, some parents do complain about subsequent behavioral changes. It's always quite shocking in today's society to see a kid reading a book.

My mom has had run-ins in the past with the parents' council for giving her students a taste for reading. The council wanted the Countess of Ségur, *The Little Prince*, and other monarchs reinstated to the curriculum. What's the point given that all young people are anarchists! You have to be ready to grab the bull by the horns, or the poor performers by the shoulders, and sit them at the front of the class so they'll pay attention. Gone are the days when big blockheads stirred up trouble from the back of the room for want of something better to do. By showing students things that interest them, my mom wins them over. Almost all her students like to read now. My mom calls the hulking teens her little birds, and, as she says so well, *she has them reading from her hand.*

MY HAND

I never say how old I am, I just hold up my fingers:

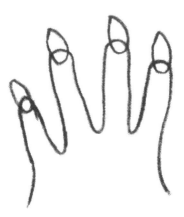

I think this is my left hand minus the thumb, not because I still suck my thumb, but because that's how old I am. I'm quite talented when I work from a model, don't you think?

You might have mistaken my fingers for lit candles if I'd been able to add colour because of my long, red nails. For that matter, my birthday is coming up soon, and there will be candles on the cake. I hope you'll come. Up until now I've always had more candles than friends, and I'd rather have it the other way round.

To tell the truth, my nails aren't red and never will be, although I do think they'd look more feminine that way. I don't have long nails, either; the subject has been a matter of great debate between my mom and me, always cut short by her. It's impossible to have the last word where she's concerned.

*

When I used to draw (I still do), I'd hold the pencil in one hand while sucking my thumb, the one on the other hand, of course. I wouldn't say a word for hours at a time, so absorbed and fascinated was I with the lines appearing on the paper under my pencil tip, lines that surely pointed to new horizons along new paths away from my witch-clad puppet hand.

You see, I have an enchanted mitten that turns my hand into a witch.

I have a puppet theatre too that my dad built, with a bit of help from me; we do everything together. The theatre is a big walk-in cardboard box with a hole cut out for your hand – I mean the puppet. It's kind of scary, but not too scary if I'm the one working the puppets.

If I'm in the audience, though, all that changes. I'm often frightened by what's hidden or in the dark. In the shadows, my hands scare me. When I can't see properly, I'm afraid. It was awful before I got my first pair of glasses. I couldn't make sense of anything – every image was blurry, muddled, insane.

I wouldn't go so far as to say that every day was black, but I never felt reassured. I don't suck my thumb anymore or suffer as much from affective disorders, probably because I started wearing glasses. I'm still scared stiff every time I go into the darkroom with my mom, though. It reminds me of my yellow bedroom in the middle of the night when I wake up and all the lights are out, except my night light projecting deformed shadows onto my ceiling. Sometimes Chlorophyll and Clarinette lie purring on my bed. I feel safe with them there, especially since cats can see in the dark.

In the faint glow of the red light, my mom's darkroom looks even more sinister, like a small cave with bats lurking inside. I don't let that stop me, though, because I love to watch the way faces and objects appear on the silver paper as my mom dunks it into a small basin full of some special liquid. The whole process is fascinating, quite magical! The transition from white to shades of black, the grey areas, the sharp images still veiled by rippling water until finally she takes the picture – smooth and wet like a cornea – out of the bath make me think of that magic moment sometime in the future when I may regain normal eyesight. In the meantime, I eat lots of carrots and hope that one day I won't need glasses anymore.

MY FRIEND

Lucienne, the friend I mentioned earlier on, is this old:

NINETY-FOUR.

Or maybe more since her age keeps on changing. I asked my dad to write the number of years down for me because I would have needed my hands, my feet, and then some to draw all those years.

Lucienne is very, very old and, of course, she wears glasses. We often go to see her because she can't see very well: she's blind, well, just about. She's just about deaf too. When you're with Lucienne, you have to enunciate very clearly and talk really loud, especially when you say the word "drawing" because she often hears "dying" instead.

Lucienne is my model. I like to capture her likeness on paper. She's easy to draw because she's the skinniest person I know and when your specialty is stick figures, the end product looks a lot closer to the original. While I draw from Lucienne, she tells me about her past, that's all she has left, and she's willing it over to me. It's important to have an inheritance when you're a princess.

Lucienne is one of my few friends. I hardly have any friends. Well actually, I hardly ever see them. I'm always alone all week long. There's my dad of course, but he's not my friend, he's my dad.

Almost all my friends, both boys and girls, go to the kindergarten down our street. All week. I'd love to go to a kinder's garden myself. I wouldn't mind not being with my dad. I'm always on his heels and that ends up getting on my nerves.

I have a full-time friend whose name is June, although I can't understand a word she says. Except when we fight over a toy, then suddenly we understand each other perfectly. Good sign language – punching and kicking and the like – says it all.

June must speak English since I can't understand a single word. She's my only day-to-day friend. Oh, I forgot! There's José and Rebecca too – unfortunately José's a boy. They both speak Spanish, and French as well. All my other friends go to kindergarten. They all speak French, even Kevin and Steven. Why that is I don't know.

There's Nino too, but he hasn't been just a friend for a long time. We're in love. We haven't French kissed yet; we're waiting for me to learn Italian so we can Italian kiss instead.

THE ISLAND

For the time being I live in Montreal, a cosmopolitan island. I like my neighbourhood and my street. My house is on Drolet. From my bedroom window you can see the crowns of trees in Carré St. Louis and, in the distance, the crowns of skyscrapers. Crowns always make a princess feel safe.

But my dad wants us to move to a desert island. We live in a city, the worst possible environment because of all the bad influences.

According to my dad, all children should be brought up in cotton batting, with sterile pads over their eyes and cotton balls stuck in their ears. Instead, my friends and I grow up on concrete, and we can see for miles. Nothing escapes our gaze. A few more trees would be a good thing, they'd keep certain sights from us. It's lucky there are so many of them in Carré St. Louis because of all the young people up to no good. I'm referring to the drug trade, of course; it's been around for as long as the world has turned and the forests have stood. We just hear about it more nowadays because of the clearcutting being done. That's all.

A SUBJECT LIKE ANY OTHER

We often hang out on a bench in Carré St. Louis. We look at the flowers for a while, then my dad writes and I play. I venture off but rarely very far because of all the big city problems. Kidnapping is an English word and it and other anglicisms roam free in Montreal. You can't walk the streets at night without running the risk of being assimilated then gagged for days or months or centuries at a time until a ransom is paid. A word of caution: you should never put anything in your mouth that comes from strangers no matter how tempting or sweet.

I'm not a racist, but I am a linguist. When a grown-up speaks to me in English, I never answer back. I don't understand a word. With June, it's not the same. She and I don't ask as many questions.

Even though my parents told her parents not to, June sometimes gives me English candy; she's an ally, I like her a lot.

On the other hand, in Carré St. Louis I meet all kinds of people to talk to.

I tell my story to anyone who'll listen. My most loyal subject is Madame Peti. I'm not kidding, that's her name, she told me so herself. I didn't believe her at first because she's not petite, she's huge. But she said it's true.

She was the first person I ever met whose name I could spell but whose picture I couldn't draw. I'm still stuck on my stick figures, you see! She glared at me for saying that, but I didn't mean to offend her.

My dad says I can talk to her, but my mom says not to touch. Madame Peti doesn't have a house; she lives in a cardboard box something like the puppet theatre my dad and I made in our basement. But it's her soaplessness not her homelessness that you notice most.

Madame Peti is very dirty, not that that means she's not nice. One mustn't discriminate amongst one's subjects; all subjects are born equal, apparently.

There's nothing wrong with being dirty, any kid can tell you that. I myself hate to be washed, especially after I've eaten. I would rather be loved instead. My dad snacks on me at snack time.

When the juice to my
cheeks kind of sticks,
my father gets in a few licks.

That's love for you. No self-respecting child likes to have a wet facecloth shoved in her face, but a spit and wash job is just plain fun. The dirtier the better. My dad doesn't bother bathing, either – baths don't turn him on.

Bath time is another matter. That's when I take my clothes off, and all hell breaks loose. It's not what you think.

I don't get clean at bath time. I have fun instead. I splash water all over the place. My dad watches me paddle, and he even plays along: we drown my rubber duckie, we sink my sailboat, we make lots of waves and noise. I even have a bubble-making gizmo, so naturally we have to add soap. We fool around until such time as there's more water on the floor than in the tub.

But let me get back to poor Madame Peti, alone in my park.

She's the one who spoke to me the first time I saw her. It's true, she actually spoke to me as though I really existed and was a full-fledged human being, not just a kid. She commented on the colour of my hair and my eyes and, of course, my clothes. She also said *How old are you, my pretty little thing?* and I showed her my usual, one hand less a thumb.

We then proceeded to have a real conversation just like grown-ups do. I tried her out on this and that, the rain, the sun, but she'd never heard of Jacques Prévert so I had to explain that *Choses et autres* and *La Pluie et le beau temps* are the titles of poems. That's when she gave me a funny look, like something was amiss. Is it that obvious? Then she asked: *Where are your parents?*

I told her they'd gone to the can because sometimes they're a pain in the ass. My answer must have reassured her that I wasn't from another planet or another time. *In my day, that kind of talk wouldn't have been allowed. Today's kids have no manners.*

How dare she insult my parents?

"What about your kids, sweetums?" I retorted.

I was exceedingly familiar with her, but not because I was brought up to be that way. I'm sure I hurt her, but I had a message to get across.

She didn't respond, at least not in words. She started to cry.

I saw that all the dirt was just a shell. For protection. Her skin must be thin and sensitive after all. Maybe she has eczema. In any case, I'd put my finger on her sore spot. Then I touched her. Literally. With my hands and my inner arms. I hugged her the best I could because Madame Peti really is huge. I wish you could have seen the picture we made, but you wouldn't have understood. I just can't draw that well.

THE FELLATIO

I'm now going to broach a topic that would be better dealt with in an adult-only book, namely sex.

I'm just kidding, I won't go there. Sex is an ongoing refrain in all novels today, even in young adult books. To tell the truth, it's become quite a hit.

Let's talk about a truly taboo subject with no place to call home, a subject that often rears its ugly head despite all precautions. I'm talking about the thorny question that is every man's nemesis, the one that makes men shudder in dread: "Daddy, where do babies come from?"

You know as well as I that any father whose little girl asks how babies are conceived – even if he's a writer with a literary reputation to uphold – won't think twice about dabbling in the sub-genre of lies. All novelists lie. The surprising part is how eager and willing they also are under those circumstances to trot out various clichés.

Believe it or not, my dad tried to make me swallow – now let me finish my sentence – that old "babies start as sweet nothings between lovers" line. Sweet nothings my eye.... Now that's a cliché if ever I heard one!

My dad dreamed up an explanation so far-fetched as to be out-of-body: *small o's dilate and turn into big O's and that's where babies come from....* Yeah, right!

There's no way I buy that.

I happen to know that to make babies you need to have a fellatio. You heard me right! Fellatio's the word I couldn't remember earlier on, the one I heard my parents mentioning to their friends.

I told my dad to quit playing dumb and to tell me all about the fellatio. Not feeling up to the task, he sent me off to speak to my mom.

I'm lucky I have my mom to tell me the facts of life. Men are well-known for their reproduction-related gaffes. At least my mom always tells the truth. Women can talk about delicate matters with each other; my mom didn't leave a thing out.

Let me explain. It's really not all that complicated.

To begin with, a fellatio is a tropical plant, a fruit-bearing tree species that produces flowers first, then small edible berries. The ripe berries, once swallowed, grow into babies in their mother's tummy.

And that's that.

I don't know if you've ever seen a fellatio berry before, but it's very colourful. A bit like me, actually.

Before reaching the edible fruit stage, the flowers themselves are quite striking. They look something like Passion flowers. Passion flowers mature into Passion fruit, often sold as juice. My mom described the flower's sexual organ for me, too. Talk about awesome. Another name for the Passion flower is *Passiflora*, and it's a member of the Passifloraceae family. It's a very special flower whose name comes from its similarity to the Passion of Christ. It has twelve sepals representing the twelve apostles, a crown of semi-erect petals resembling the crown of thorns Jesus wore, five stamens like Christ's five wounds, and three stigmas like the three nails. I think that about covers it. I'd love to draw the flower for you, but I wouldn't be able to do it justice.

Of course, given the way my dad feels about religion, he would never eat a Passion flower.

So there you are, I'm the fruit of a fellatio, and I'm good enough to eat. I'm so cute you'd swear sometimes my dad thinks I have no brains. Honestly, what does he take me for, trying to mystify me with his story of O and capital O's at that! My dad lives in a fantasy world and thinks I should too. Next he'll be telling me that old wives' tale about babies in the cabbage patch when everyone knows only slugs are born there.

THE MAGAZINE

I stole a kid's magazine. Have you ever heard of toys by Playskool? Well then, I'm sure you've heard of magazines by *Playboy!*

Sometimes we go as a family to browse at the newspaper store that sells books and magazines too. Of course, my mom makes a beeline for the section on gardening, photography, and education. My dad could use an intensive dose of the latter as well; education is important.

Instead he heads for the fluff magazines.

Inside the store, he hoists me up on his shoulders so I won't get into anything. During our last outing, his precautions were useless since I managed to grab a magazine from the upper stand and discreetly slide it under my sweater.

What a shoplifting feat!

Back home, I turned pages without reading a one and so, naturally, I didn't fall asleep. The activity was highly instructive for the woman-in-waiting I am. I'm a future mother after all; just like my mom I want children.

It turns out that the magazine was about kids,

not for them. The overarching theme was clearly motherhood. All the mothers were naked, and the interview with each young mother was illustrated with a series of explicit photographs. Some showed balloon-breasted mothers most likely getting ready to nurse and others lying prone in the delivery position.

Luckily my dad came into my bedroom and saw me with the magazine, so I had an opportunity to ask him a few questions since he knows how to read so well.

My dad, commonly known as a man, didn't let being outnumbered by women make him turn tail. He tackled every one, no matter how delicate. He didn't miss a trick; every single question was answered, and they really were delicate. Questions are known to be a parent's worst enemy.

The questions won't be reproduced here because reproducing the list of all my questions for my dad would mean this wouldn't be a normal book, but a questionnaire.

That day, all my nascent career plans were nipped in the bud. I finally knew what I want to do when I grow up: I want to pose.

Pose questions of course.

THE INTERVIEW

I'd really like to be a reporter. Since my change in career plans, my dad has introduced me to several reporters. I just happened to be along for all the press interviews he's done recently and felt an instant rapport with the people asking my dad incessant questions.

The latest one was a radio interview, but my dad took me with him anyway.

He wanted to leave me with the producer as soon as we got to the studio, but the producer had other plans; she had no idea what a production my presence would be. She thought I'd just accompany my dad. I was so cute the on-air host fell for me too the minute she laid eyes on me. I don't think my dad trusts hosts and that's why he doesn't send me to church.

My dad kept trying to object, but to no avail. The producer had the last word just like every other woman in my dad's life.

I sat in a huge chair wearing a headset that was way too big for me and engulfed both sides of my head. I'm sure I must have looked like a sandwich.

I could hear everything people said in the studio while we were on air.

My dad was careful to tell me not to say a word, but I lost my resolve when the host turned to me to ask a few questions.

My dad had mentioned that the broadcast would be live, and it's true the questions were all about my life: *How does your daddy treat you? Does he play with you a lot? Did he used to change your diaper when you were little? What do the two of you do all day? In short, what kind of a relationship do you and your daddy have?*

"Purely sexual!"

My dad is still mad at me for my quip, but my mom always cracks up whenever she tells the story.

GRANDPARENTS

My dad doesn't take me along on interviews any-more. He has me babysat. He doesn't plant me in the kindergarten down our street, though; he drops me off at my grandparents' instead.

I like my grandparents a lot. They're always so nice. They take me for walks in the park and let me ask them delicate questions they can't answer – they pretend they're out of breath.

They're speechless because my dad has strictly forbidden them from scolding me for telling them about the birds and the bees and the jesus bugs. Flowers attract all kinds, what else can I say?

My grandparents wait on me hand and foot. Being babysat at their house is like a fairy tale, a real one along the lines of Aladdin and his wonderful lamp or Ali Baba and the forty flying carpet thieves who stole all kinds of other things too, all of which are hidden away at my grandparents' for them to present me with as gifts. They fulfill all my wishes, but I'm entitled to more than three since they satisfy my every whim. My grandparents are the ones who gave me the videos of Ali Baba and Aladdin, such a charming macho that one, a champion mounted on his marching camel in hot pursuit of Princess Jasmina for love's sake, probably because they haven't had children yet. What a great story! I never fall asleep while it's on.

My dad doesn't want me playing the videos at home anymore, so he put the two videos on consignment at my grandpa's. At Grandpa's, I can watch them as much as I want and sit on his lap while stuffing my face with homemade ice cream. What a blast! My grandparents are real softies.[7] Especially Grandpa. He loves me as much as my own dad does, maybe even more. He lets me do what I please and have what I want, except for candy. That's because my dad strictly forbids it. My dad can't stand to see me spoiled.

7   It's unclear whether the author means "soft touch" or "soft in the head." In any case both are disrespectful. Correctrix's note.

WAR

My dad would let me be a reporter, but no way would he let me work for a major. He hates the army, you see. That's why he won't let me go to kindergarten down the street, or anywhere else that would provide the education the majors seek.

My dad doesn't want to see me end up in a barracks or, worse still, area headquarters, anymore than he wants me to go to the area school in September. It's too far away. Plus, school's too regimented anyway.

My dad knows whereof he speaks. As incredible as this may sound, he went to school when he was young and joined the Canadian Armed Forces when he was dumb.

I won't be making the same mistakes; my dad will see to that.

When I grow up, one thing I do know is that I'll live on a princely estate.

Down the street from us stands a real castle. Not a word of a lie, an honest-to-goodness castle you can see for yourself on the corner of Des Pins and Drolet.

It's a huge stone building with towers and crenelles like teeth but no machicolations. In the fortress live enemies whom my dad and I despise. Dangerous enemies whom we'd gladly kill. That's the way of the world: where you have castles, you're bound to have wars and assassinations. I know fighting's bad, but that's life.

I often launch attacks on their impregnable stronghold. Every time my dad and I walk past, I throw rocks. What I really need is a catapult, or at least a slingshot like the ones for sale at the convenience store, but my dad won't buy me one. It's too dangerous for my eyes.

Inside the castle is a rankery, a real one. And rankery is the right word, don't go thinking the correctrix got it wrong. You know full well that no correctrix has proofed my dad's book.

The rankery is where big kids go to change their rank, of course. Rankery and nursery sound alike, but a nursery's for infants and a rankery's for infantry. You heard right, infantry, the word really does exist! An infantry's infants have their own special name: they're called foot soldiers. Foot soldiers are even worse than ordinary kids. These ones shoot to kill. Which is why they have to be stopped before the other infants get hurt.

PEACE

No wars ever break out in my park though. The only gathering of the troops is for Peace and Love. All my troops ever do is smoke dope and play guitar. So we too play in peace.

Carré St. Louis is a good place to play; in fact, once my dad and I saw Monique Spaziani there. She's not just a character, she's a real actress and she was playing quietly with a baby. Which goes to show that it's not just the stage or the screen that has important roles up for grabs.

MONDAY

SUMMER

Today is the first day of summer holidays.

What a way to start them!

Remember the shoe I stole? We were supposed to take it back on Saturday, but the store closed before we got there so now we're going back today. Talk about starting off on the wrong foot!

"But the shoe's gone, Daddy. I threw it into someone's eye, and now it will probably be used as an exhibit at my trial! There's no point going back to the store now."

We're going back to pay for that shoe. My dad was not in a good mood, so I quit arguing.

We stood outside the store.

Believe you me, I was squirming in my shoes. Somehow I had to figure out how to talk my way out of this one.

We walked inside.

To begin with, my dad recounted Saturday's events to the saleswoman; she distinctly remembered the mayhem out on the street. My dad pointed out that the reason the incident took place in front of her store was that my mom and I were on our way there.

The encounter was going smoothly, but my dad, in his naiveté, had to go spoil it all by mentioning why we were on our way back to the store last Saturday.

Imagine what that made me look like!

A thief, that's what!

With the clerk's eyes on me, I began to play up my cuteness and told her "the story about the coach that changes into a pumpkin and the ball the princess flees, just about breaking her neck on the stairs, but luckily she got away with a twisted ankle, although she did lose the damn shoe, which is why my mom for one never wears high heels and never goes to balls." As you can well imagine, I was a shoe-in. The store clerk couldn't bring herself to call the police. I was just too cute as a thief and a story-teller so she said she'd wipe the slate clean.

But my dad would have none of any half-assed cleaning job. He insisted, saying there was a lesson to be learned and that he had to make me pay for the shoe from my own savings. *Oh, don't do that, sir! Leave be, your little girl didn't mean any harm, poor thing, give her back her piggybank* and so on and so forth.

In his naiveté, my dad left a considerable quantity of large coins next to the cash register anyway and together we made tracks out of there, so fast that my feet hardly touched the ground the way my dad was pulling on my arm. The saleswoman followed at a trot, saying again how she didn't want the money and how I was just too cute, but my dad forged ahead. The saleswoman stopped at the door.

The episode was over. Soon the street noise drowned out the saleswoman's protests, and a radiant sun shone down. The End.

*

Today is the first day of summer holidays because when we got back, my mom was still at home. Usually on a Monday, she'd have left for school by now. She won't be teaching today and once more, it won't be today that I learn how to read.

My mom won't be going to school tomorrow either, or the day after or for many sleeps after that. Summer is here.

My dad isn't on holidays because he never works. As I mentioned already, my dad's a *wrrriter*, but that's not the way it's pronounced. Only Françoise is allowed to roll her r's that much. She's French from France, and she doesn't sound that way to put on airs; you can take my word for it, she really comes from France.

France is big on colonizing, but it never colonized me since my dad would never let me roll my r's like Françoise because it's bad for my mother tongue.

Incredible but true, France is also my cousin's first name.

I can't stand my cousin!

France is older than I am. I don't know how old because I'd need more than my two hands put together. Maybe my feet would do the trick, but I don't know how to count on my toes.

I don't like France.

She knows how to read, that cow. *Merde alors!*

It's not fair. She won't teach me. It's not like she wouldn't have had time the other day when she came over with her parent, she did, but no, not her, she wanted to draw with my felt pens. Jesus Christ!

I don't mince my words, of that you can be sure. My dad's responsible for my vocabulary. I hear things first, then I repeat them. I don't make them up.

So today is Monday, and my mom is staying home with us. "Us" includes Françoise because Monday is cleaning day. After the weekend, there's always stuff lying all over the house.

Zees bedroom ees a fucking mess!

That's what she says, but it's not as bad as all that. I understand Françoise perfectly, even her unholy swears, because I for one wouldn't want to have to restore order to this mess.

THE NURSERY

I'm going to the nursery today.

Even though my dad's at home, as long as I'm little, every Monday, or just about, I have to go to the nursery. I have no choice.

Parents who send their children to a nursery must never have had to go themselves when they were kids because if they had, they would never subject their children to the same treatment.

In the nursery, we learn English words like hamburger, hot dog, and Jell-O, none of them made for my tongue. So much for our menu. Often our activities aren't any better. You can only play doctor for so long before you get sick.

I don't understand how parents can leave their children alone at the nursery in Intensive Care.

On a daily basis, it makes no sense!

You have to be really sick to go to a nursery. It's not my fault that I'm a diabetic.

A nursery like mine has nurses to look after us. Nurse Claudette, Nurse Monique, Nurse Hélène, and several others whose names I don't know. My nurse's name is Nurse Francine. She takes good care of me.

Nurse Francine helps me to get my meals, to get dressed, and to make my bed once in a while. She plays board games with me and even braids my hair sometimes.

So a nursery has nurses: RN's, LPN's, VON's and, inevitably, no see'ems. Those are the ones I hate! Their hypocrisy knows no bounds. They flash hyena grins showing sharp canines, then make me look the other way, only to take a bite as soon as my head is turned! I turn back to discover it was a shot. They make me sick!

Take it from me, no medication will ever cross these lips! I'm not like the other kids who get theirs in chewable tablets or a syrup. My medication comes in a needle. How many people do you know who like to have a needle jabbed into them? Nobody, although most people put up with it. They'd have to put me to sleep to get my go-ahead, but then it would never end.

I think I already told you that my dad says all children should be raised in cotton batting, with sterile pads over their eyes and cotton balls stuck in their ears. That's why we often make the trip to the *cleeneeque* as Françoise calls it, but we call it the nursery.

To my dad and me, the word *hospital* doesn't mean anything anymore; we've banished it from our vocabulary. Whenever we go, we tell everyone we're off to the nursery and that way everyone thinks I'm normal. But if I were really like everyone else, things would be different and I'd go to the kindergarten down our street. But my dad wouldn't send me there for all the tea in China. He loves me too much to abandon me all day long.

When I sleep over at the nursery (it happens sometimes), my parents come to read me my bedtime story, and my mom always brings flowers, which I love. The other day she brought some chrysanthemums, dahlias, zinnias, gladiola, and sweet myosotis, which means "forget me not." Some people claim it's a flower for funerals, but you shouldn't pay attention to what other people say. All flowers exude both pollen and joy.

JULY

THE PARTY

Today is my birthday.

I'm a big girl now, but I don't have a big decorated cake. I've actually never had a birthday cake, the kind full of sucrose and saccharose and covered in coloured icing that other kids revel in at my friends' birthday parties as I look on enviously. I don't go to those parties anymore because those store-bought cakes are just too tough.

Candles are another matter. I always have candles, more and more every year. This year, for example, I think I have as many candles as fingers on my right hand.

My parents used to stick them in a cinnamon bun they special ordered from the baker who knew of my intolerance. Cinnamon isn't sweet, and I'm allowed as much as I want. I savoured those cinnamon buns up until the day I was allowed to eat a strawberry charlotte that my dad made himself following strict dietary guidelines.

Since then it's become my official dessert.

This year there's another surprise waiting for me. I still don't know what it is. All I know is that the surprise isn't here in the house, that it's somewhere else and that we have to drive to a secret place.

The bad part is I always fall asleep in the car: the minute my parents whisk me in, I'm out.

I hope my present is a reading lesson.

I'd love to have a present that's not a thing. After all, I can always shoplift things. A lesson in reading, on the other hand, is a lot harder to steal.

I would so love a reading lesson. I think I'm old enough now.

Maybe the final destination for our car ride will be the school. My mom's a teacher, and she has the key. I just bet that's what my present is. It would be so wicked to learn to read and write.

STOLEN TIME

Eye travel with my pair ants.

I'm practising for high school. Homophones are a teen's worst enemy according to my mom, and I want to be prepared.

My mom teaches French and yet, guess what my birthday present is. A trip! What kind of present is that for a little girl like me when it's a French lesson I need!

Anyhow, this summer we're going to France. It's like unprofessional development for my mom.

I really wanted a French lesson as a gift, and now it looks as though I'm going to have to figure out how to steal one.

A trip…

My parents still travel, even with me they still want to see the world. My presence means they have to make certain concessions. Not that many, though. In France, for instance, we're going to visit the châteaux. This is the part of the trip that's my birthday present.

My parents are selfish. They have only their own interests at heart, otherwise we'd be going to the

Wonderful World of Disney in Florida. But no, of course not, we're going to France and you can bet there'll be châteaux, red and white: Château-Margaux, Château-Latour, Château-Cheval, and several other châteaux I've heard mentioned at length. My parents are downright alcoholics; they drink wine the way I drink milk.

But don't worry about me, we'll also visit some real châteaux too, like the ones in fairy tales because they put me to sleep and that way my parents can eat and drink in peace come night! Our tours of medieval castles will suit them just fine. They know I'll be down for the count by the time we're through. Maybe even earlier. Then you can bet they'll be stuffing their faces and downing their booze in peace!

I bet we hit every château going. It's enough to make you sick – there have to be hundreds of them over there.

*

I can't wait for us to land.

I didn't mention this, but we're on a plane. I say "we," but you don't have to come. I don't have a choice. I have to go everywhere with my parents.

Was I right or was I right! I fell asleep in the car and when I woke up, we were on this plane.

I've been afraid of planes ever since my dad told me what happened to the airplane pilot who used to write books while he flew. Naturally his aircraft crashed – in the desert – and I'm afraid the same thing will happen to ours.

My dad has promised we won't be crossing any deserts.

THE LITTLE PRINCE

Speaking of which, for several nights in a row my dad read me a story called *The Little Prince*. Aside from Prévert's collection, it was the first time my dad read a book that lightweight to me. It's called a pocket book. Usually, he reads to me from big hardcover tomes that I have a hard time holding on my own. But this one was a cinch to hold.

The story's okay, but the little boy obviously comes from another planet and sees life through rose-coloured glasses.

Other than that, it's a good book.

That first night, I didn't fall asleep until almost halfway through the book, in large part thanks to the effective narrative structure, the seamless use of dialogue and the illustrations, especially the grey sheep. My dad counted them for me every night, but I never closed my eyes during that part. It was too early. It does take several pages, you know, for me to fall asleep.

As I think I've already mentioned, every night my dad starts back at the beginning of the story he began the night before, which means I never know the ending, except in real baby books with hardly any pages.

My dad says that beginnings are of the utmost importance, and that you have to glean everything you can from them in order to understand what happens later on, unless, I suppose, you're able to read the whole thing in one sitting, which would be ideal.

But back to gathering wool.

My dad read the beginning of *The Little Prince* for almost a whole month before I got tired of it and asked for another story. Every night he read and read and read, and I never fell asleep until the chapter with a drawing of what must be Victor-Lévy Beaulieu.[8]

The fact that I can stay awake that long is a testament to the quality of the writing. I do, however, have one serious complaint. The writing is too small. It almost looks like poetry.

So I asked my dad if he could do a better job for me since it really was too miniscule for my liking. Even if I could read, I don't think I would have been able to decipher all the words, given my poor eyesight.

Since my dad loves me big time, he said right away: *Of course, princess.*

---

8   We saw Victor-Lévy Beaulieu at Trois-Pistoles last month, and Charlotte was very impressed by his big beard and big hat. Saint-Exupéry's drawing in Chapter XII does in fact resemble the author from the south shore of our St. Lawrence. Author's note.

READING

We're in Paris now, Perrault's homeland, and, as incredible as it may seem, I love it! Even though I still can't read, even though my afternoon nap has taken on alarming dimensions, this place is heaven!

Every night, in a dark room on the third floor of a small no-star hotel in France, a miracle occurs! Unless it's some kind of new chemical reaction.

Every night at bedtime, my parents still administer a story to me, but the stories have lost their soporific properties! Incredible but true! For several days now, I've been able to hear The End without passing out first.

I just don't understand.

I'm not tired when my dad reads to me, not in the least. Fascinating, isn't it? Have the narcotic properties of great literature worn off? Have I finally reached the last irreversible stage of addiction?

Whatever the case, I now note that fairy tales often end with the following sentence: *They lived happily every after and had many children.*

Why is it that almost all tales finish so evasively?

Most adults who write fairy tales part-time are full-time parents and know full well the hairy adventures they'd have to recount if they didn't end their stories with the birth of their offspring. I should know.

In my opinion, that's exactly why they cut their tales short.

Personally, I would be curious to know how the books' protagonists cope with their progeny. We never see the interaction between the children and all those kings in love with queens, all those princes kissing sleeping princesses and ringless knights seeking ringletted damsels in distress. There's no way the characters' lives grind to a halt the day they exchange rings!

Whenever my parents recite *they had many children*, I think to myself, it figures, just when the action's getting good!

I stamp my feet and wait impatiently for the story to continue.

It never does. Instead I'm told my story's over, and it's time for me to go to sleep. No! I won't sleep! I insist even more loudly on having another story read right to the very end. I cry, I scream, I make a scene!

It's always when the story ends that the action begins.

*

Unfortunately, my dad is quite impervious to my vocal demonstrations. You'd think the man didn't love me. When he's decided it's bedtime, there are no ifs or buts. I can keep yelling – he won't care. We're in a little Parisian hotel room, but my dad couldn't give a damn about the other guests. He'd let me yell all night, even if I woke up the whole third floor, or maybe even the whole eleventh.[9]

---

9   Eleventh arrondissement, a district in Paris. Author's note.

REALITY

Certain episodes in this book refer to actual events and real people. I've named them all. They're my friends.

Other people may have recognized themselves in this story, especially since I haven't drawn them. Similar novelistic situations occur in several families, or what remains of them.

Grown-ups do what they can. Parenting is not an easy job. With children the great saga begins, so I understand the occasional desire to shut one's eyes.

In my case, fairy tales put me to sleep.

CASTLES

As planned, we visited scores of castles. I saw real armour, shields, crossbows, cannons and cannon-balls, swabs (it's true), antique furniture, ancient tapestries, guillotines for crimes of horror, scaffolding for necks to hang, and children's thrones. In those days, they cut off royal children's heads; my nightmares have just gotten worse. My dad's the one who suffers the most when I wake up at night because it's his job to look after me. My mom has had a year's worth of children keeping her awake during the day; she doesn't need a summer full of sleepless nights as well.

The castles house replicas of sceptres, daggers, slings, swords, restored queens' crowns, medieval gadgets, slide shows on castle life, and, to be perfectly honest, I was royally bored. You couldn't touch a thing or speak too loudly because of the guides who spoke too softly, it was too hot, I was always thirsty, it took too long to go pee, and on and on. A real nightmare…

According to my parents, however, on my wedding night I'll have forgotten all that. In fact, the thought of my getting married worries them the most.

My parents would rather go to a funeral than a wedding.

They've lost too many friends who decided to link their fate to the Church's. In fact, I think it's going to be Claudine's turn to marry soon; it's a shame because I liked her a lot.

On the other hand, my dad and mom have an excellent relationship with people who've been buried, notwithstanding the priest and the final rites.

My parents don't believe in God. I can't stress that fact enough.

More than marriage, my dad worries that I'll discover I have a vocation. He told me in no uncertain terms that he'd disown me if I succumbed! He'd never come to visit me in the convent. He would rather see me kill someone and visit me in prison than hear me saying how everyone's so nice and sweet and forgiving people their every transgression.

He does, however, think he can impart his solid spiritual values to me. In any case, he says my chances of joining a convent are as good as my chances of one day publishing a book without telling the publisher whose daughter I am. On the other hand, if I never take my vows, he has promised to throw wide open the doors to any publishing house, if that's what I want. His promise hasn't fallen on deaf ears. Who knows, maybe some day I will finally learn to read and write?

THE ZOO

As always, the holidays have gone by too fast.

The next and last stage of our trip through France is the Vincennes zoological park in Paris.

We've made a special trip just for me, and I'm expecting the worst. There will be lions, tigers, and black panthers, ferocious carnivores every one; rhinoceri with horns on their snouts and elephants with trunks for strangling. Although they're said to be nice, I'll wait and see. We'll see hyenas that prey on the small and the weak, crocodiles, tarantulas, and poisonous snakes, not to mention parrots that might repeat every word I say. That too is very dangerous.

It's not that I question my parents' love for me, but when you look at all the names they've called me over the years, I worry that they're trying to get rid of me.

I heard them talking the other night. We're going to be taking another plane soon. My parents will ask for the window seat and, if I understood correctly, I'll be left on the outside.

I'm going to have to learn French slang since I'll be living in Paris from here on in.

I'm afraid that the purpose of this trip to the zoo is an excuse for a delivery and that I'm the package to be dropped off!

That's because, as I already mentioned, my parents have always had very strange names for their little girl. I've been treated to every animal name in the book, each one preceded by the same adjective. I've been called every name imaginable without a thought on my parents' part to how ridiculous, how clichéd, how redundant they might sound. My little kitten, my little mouse, my little lion, my little dove, my little red love squirrel, my little rabbit, my little lamb, my little tadpole, etc.

But when we have people over, I'm always just their princess.

THE TRIP HOME

The holidays sure went by fast. Orléans, Blois, Amboise, Poitiers, Royan, Bordeaux, Biarritz, Pau, Toulouse, Carcassonne, Béziers, Sète, Montpellier, Nîmes, Arles, and Marseille, and I'm still no better in French since I can't read or write, but now I'm a whiz in geography. We also passed through Lourdes, but I'm still a diabetic.

Everything went by too fast.

As it turned out, my parents didn't leave me behind at the zoo.

We're in the plane.

We're going home.

SEPTEMBER

SCHOOL

Today is the last day of summer.

And the last day of sunshine. Tomorrow it's going to rain. Tomorrow I go to school since my dad never got around to teaching me how to read. At bedtime tonight, he recited a poem he'd learned by heart.

The violins
of autumn
pierce
my heart
in long laments.
My heart weeps
like rain
falling.
What mournful air
cloaks my heart?

The poem didn't work because it wasn't long enough despite the late hour. It didn't even move me, I didn't close my eyes or yawn.

My dad really doesn't want me to go to school. I can tell by the way his eyes fill with drops, and I even heard a tremor in his voice. He's going to want to keep me with him tomorrow morning, I can tell. He's not going to want to let me go. I can tell just by the way he's hugging me tonight. Tighter than usual.

Since the poem wasn't enough to put me to sleep, my dad read me my story from a book. There once was a princess who gardened and reigned over *Helianthus*, also known as sunflowers. She had all kinds of adventures, but flowers were her passion until the very end. The sunflowers were gigantic and their joy contagious as it radiated throughout the garden all season long. The story more or less ended on that note, and my dad said *good night, princess* then kissed me on my forehead.

Tonight my dad read me my story for the very last time. As of tomorrow, I won't need either him or my mom anymore. Tomorrow morning, I'm finally going to school, my mom promised, and I'll learn to read that afternoon. I won't need my parents to read to me anymore. I'll know how to read myself. Tomorrow.

THE END

"Daddy! Daddy! I can't get to sleep…."

BIBLIOGRAPHICAL REFERENCES

Several pages in this book first appeared as a short story in July 1997 in the newspaper *Le Devoir*.

The Kite, reproduced on page 65, is a tale written by Martine Théberge (my other half).

Patience is a virtue for those who don't realize how desperately short life is. This sentence quoted on page 68 comes from the text entitled *Ode to Impatience* by Hubert Aquin.

If there's one thing I can't stand in life, it's my mother (page 99) is the opening line in Flora Balzano's novel *Soigne ta chute*.

This book
set in Palatino 12 on 14.5
was printed
in August 2000
at Imprimerie Gauvin,
Hull (Québec).